MW01008068

HELEN HARDT

Her Two Lovers

A COLLECTION OF MÉNAGE ROMANCE

Copyright © 2017 Waterhouse Press, LLC
Cover Design by Waterhouse Press, LLC
Cover Photographs: Ingimage

Paperback ISBN: 978-1-943893-50-8

Her Two Lovers

A COLLECTION OF MÉNAGE ROMANCE

WATERHOUSE PRESS

Loving Eve

CHAPTER ONE

Jon Blake had long, thick fingers, and each time Eve saw them she imagined them sliding in and out of her pussy. Mmm, stretching and massaging, nice slow burn. His lips were full and dark red. What woman wouldn't kill for lips like those? They should be classified as lethal weapons as far as Eve was concerned. More than once she'd gotten herself off to the image of them clamped around her hard nipple, sucking and tugging.

Jon was a dark-haired, dark-eyed mountain of a man, all broad shoulders and ripped muscle. A personal trainer, he was six feet and three inches of pure masculinity. A vivid image of his magnificent body bound for her pleasure skated into her mind.

Eve shimmied her shoulders, erasing the image, and the coins on her shiny onyx bra jingled and sparkled. Her ample breasts shook with the rhythm and nearly spilled from captivity.

For Jon. He was a self-professed boob man. She removed a sapphire veil from her hips and wrapped it around Jon's thick neck.

Then she turned to Brian. Brian Conrad's auburn hair suited his green eyes and fair complexion. He was as gorgeous as Jon, but in a completely different way. A pianist, he boasted fingers that were beautifully slender...and amazingly nimble. From Chopin to Rachmaninoff to the jazzy blues of

Thelonious Monk, Brian's fingers danced across the ivories with soul searing motivation.

Eve's skin heated as a vivid scene floated into her mind. Her, lying on a bed, while Brian stripped her slowly, languidly, and then played her body like his instrument, starting softly with kisses and caresses and crescendoing to *fortissimo* as he thrust into her welcoming cunt.

She tickled his chiseled jaw with a veil, teal this time, slid it around his neck, and fluttered her belly.

Brian loved belly flutters. Said they were the sexiest moves he'd ever seen. They required control of the diaphragm and were difficult to master. Eve was famous for her flutters, and she loved sharing them with Brian. He made no secret that she had the sexiest tummy and rear end he'd ever seen.

She rewarded him with a quick hip shimmy and belly roll before she moved on to the next table, her hips swaying to the melodic chords of the acoustic guitar, the haunting strains of the violin, and the clear, hollow resonance of the flute. Underneath the melody and harmony, the mellow cadence of the *dumbek* provided a brisk rhythm, and Eve circled her hips in time with the beat. She danced to the center of the restaurant as the music of the guitar, violin, and flute faded away.

Time for her drum solo. She eyed the *dumbek* player. Damn, he was good-looking too. Had the Oasis Restaurant only admitted gorgeous men tonight? A sea of raw male beauty splashed around her.

Handsome as the drummer was, though, this dance was for Jon and Brian. All her dances were for Jon and Brian. Her two biggest fans. Her two best friends. She nodded her head slightly, and the drummer began. Her head bowed, her brown hair tickling her shoulders in soft waves, she began with a freeze, shifting her heels in short rapid movements against the floor. Only a glimmer of vibration touched her hips and tummy, but it was enough to get her audience hooting for more.

She raised her head and smiled her most brilliant smile. She snaked one arm behind her neck and held up her cascading hair while she circled her chest, and then her hips, in opposite directions. Gazing around the semi-circular room, she made eye contact with all the guests, men and women alike. Once she knew they were with her, she fell into a whole-body undulation and gave herself over to the *dumbek*.

The audience was gone then. Nothing existed except the *dumbek*, Eve and the dance.

And Jon and Brian, of course. Somehow, they were always there, inside her.

She gyrated her hips in a slow figure eight, four drum beats to every pulse of her body. Then two, and then one, until she was oscillating twice to every beat. The tempo throbbed through her and soon the beat was a part of her, calling her to the dance. No longer did she think about her moves. She simply felt, leaping inside the music as it swirled through her veins in a heady pattern of poetry and rhythm.

Silver waves of nearly visible energy surged through her and heated her skin. Her nipples tightened against her glittery bra, and her pussy thrummed along with the *dumbek*. Tiny electric sparks skittered over her flesh. Her muscular legs kept pace under her frothy skirts, and she flashed one every several beats. Her bare feet ground into the carpeted stage as she twirled her skirts, spiraled her body, shook her hips and chest. Her skirts flowed, her coins jingled, her hair swayed, drifting over the bare skin of her back and shoulders in silky caresses.

She made love through the dance. That, her reviewers

said, was what made her the most popular belly dancer in the state of Arizona.

When the drummer signaled her, she executed a succession of rapid turns and fell to the ground in a perfect backbend.

Applause thundered through the restaurant, and Eve waited a moment, perspiration beading on her forehead, before she rose, stood tall, smiled, and bowed.

The flute and guitar played a lively tune and she sashayed around to each table. The patrons generously stuffed tips into her shimmery belt. She acknowledged each customer with grace and a smile.

"One more round of applause for the lovely Evonna!"

She whirled to center stage and bowed again. Dollar bills drifted from her waistband. The restaurant manager would collect them for her.

When the applause died down, she smiled once more then made her way to the corner table Jon and Brian occupied. They both stood.

Jon leaned over to kiss her cheek. She quivered from the press of his full, dark lips and the scraping of his scruffy stubble.

Brian, more formal and gentlemanly, kissed her fingertips, and a series of little quakes surged through her.

They were so wonderful. Her best friends in the universe.

How could she be in love with both of them?

Oh, but she was. Had been for a while. They'd met in college and now shared a loft in downtown Tucson. When they decided to live together, they'd agreed to keep their relationship platonic. Both Jon and Brian had made it clear they considered her a friend and nothing more. Two years ago she was right there with them.

But now? She'd fallen head over heels for them both. How had she let this happen? A woman couldn't love two men, could she? What kind of loose floozy did that make her?

She sat down and wiped her sweating face and chest with a cloth napkin. Not real ladylike, but she was sopping wet. Her chestnut hair stuck to her cheeks in strands. Dancing was wonderful exercise and she loved every minute of it. But she sweated like a pig afterwards.

"You need a drink, honey?" Jon pushed his water glass toward her.

"You're an angel." Eve took a long gulp. Pure nectar.

"That was one of your best shows ever." Brian winked. "Lots of flutters."

Eve swallowed and let out a giggle. "You know I'd never disappoint you, Bri."

Jon cleared his throat and opened his mouth.

Brian furrowed his brow. "Not now, bud."

Hmm. Something was up. "Not now what?"

"Yes, damn it." Jon pounded a fist on the table.

Eve jerked in her chair. "Jon, are you okay?"

"I'm fine." He shook his head. "Aw, hell. That's a lie. I'm not fine, and neither is Bri. We've got ourselves one giant problem, honey."

They were in trouble? Her heart lurched. "What can I do to help?"

"Nothing," Jon said. "You're the problem, see?"

"Me?" Eve squirmed in her chair. "What have I done?"

"Ignore him, sweetheart," Brian said, his deep voice soothing. "You haven't done anything. That's not what he meant."

"What exactly do you mean then, Jon?"

"Well...Brian and I...we... Aw, shit." He thunked his forehead to the table, his sable hair spilling across the linen cloth in a mass of beautiful waves.

"Nice, bud. Real nice." Brian shook his head. "Look, sweetheart, we don't want to upset you, but there is something you need to know."

"What?" Eve trembled. "Is one of you in trouble or something?"

"No, nothing like that," Brian said. "It's just, in the past few months, Jon and I have discovered..."

Eve balanced on the edge of her seat. "Discovered what?"

Jon raised his head, and his dark eyes burned into hers. "We're in love with you, Eve. Both of us are totally and completely in love with you."

Eve stood, knocking her chair backward.

"Great job, dude," Brian said. "Now you've freaked her out. That's perfect."

Jon gestured to the waiter at the next table. "I need a stiff martini, extra dry."

"Make that two," Brian said and turned back to Jon. "We could have done this later, you know. Anywhere but in the middle of a crowded restaurant after she's just done a show. The poor thing's exhausted."

In love with her? Both of them? What was she supposed to do with that? And now they were talking about her as if she weren't even there!

"I'm sorry, honey," Jon said. "Do you want a drink? A margarita or something?"

A margarita, her favorite drink. They both knew her so well. But a drink was the last thing she needed. She shook her head, stepped over her chair, and headed to the ladies' room.

Once there, she turned on the faucet and splashed cold water on her face. The icy zing soothed her heated skin like a minty salve.

In love with her.

Now what? She eyed her face in the mirror. Drips of the cool water mingled with lingering trickles of perspiration. Plain gray eyes, a slightly too-long nose. Her hair was nice—long, thick, and wavy—though it was an unmemorable brown. Pink lips, but not full enough. She'd kill for Jon's lips.

She wasn't anything special. Not like the two of them were. How could they both have fallen for her? She twirled in front of the mirror, creating a breeze that, coupled with the water and perspiration, helped cool her scorching body. Her body. Well, she did have a smokin' body. Dancing definitely had its benefits. Still, the idea of Jon and Brian, two perfect male specimens, in love with her was... Flattering, yes. Amazing. A complete turn-on, since she loved them both with all her soul.

But wedged in the happiness was heartbreak as well. How had it happened? How could she deal with this? She took a deep breath, left the ladies' room, and returned to the table.

"Honey," Jon said, "I'm so sorry. I didn't mean to upset you."

"What do you want me to do?" she asked.

"Do... you have feelings for either one of us? Or do you think you could, ever? In the future maybe?"

"Of course. I love you both. You know that." More than they knew. More than she thought they could ever know. Now, could she possibly have one of them? As more than a friend? How would she choose?

"It's like this," Jon said. "You're going to have to choose."

"Dear Lord." Heat flashed over her, and she grabbed the

glass of water and took a deep swallow. "Choose? I haven't said I want either of you."

But she did. She wanted them both. With a fierce passion that smoldered between her legs at that very moment.

"Give us each a chance," Brian said.

"Give you a chance? This is insanity." She let out a frustrated sigh. "And what happens to the one I don't choose?"

"Bri and I have agreed to stay friends, no matter what," Jon said, "haven't we?"

Brian cleared his throat. "Yeah. We have. It'll be hard, but we've been friends too long to let a woman come between us."

"But I never wanted to come between you at all!"

"We know, honey," Jon said, "but we can't help the way we feel. Would you be willing?"

"To what? Date you? Both of you?"

Brian sighed and smiled a weak smile. "Well...yeah, I guess. To get to know both of us in a romantic sort of way."

Jon let out a breath. "We know it's kind of an unusual request."

"Unusual? Try completely crazy."

Neither Jon nor Brian spoke. They simply looked at her, stared at her, until four beautiful eyes, two dark and two green, burned into her heart like flaming arrows.

Finally, Jon narrowed his gaze. "Are you attracted to either one of us? In that way?"

Uh, yeah. Completely hot and horny for you both, thank you very much. She fidgeted with the coins draping her breasts. They tinkled above the din of the restaurant. She lowered her head, unable to meet their penetrating gazes. "Yes," she said softly. "I'm attracted to you. To both of you." She raised her head and looked first at Jon, and then Brian. "You're gorgeous, amazing. You have wonderful hearts. I dearly love you both. How can I possibly choose one of you? How can you ask this of me?"

"Believe me, sweetheart"—Brian took her hand and lightly massaged her palm—"if there were any other way, we'd do it. But we're both crazy in love with you, Eve. If there's a possibility you could feel the same way about one of us, the other could never take away that chance for ultimate happiness."

Jon nodded. "Bri and I have talked about this, honey. We figured the only fair way was for both of us to woo you."

"And what if I don't choose either of you?"

"Then at least we tried," Brian said. "Right now, we're both suffering. Maybe one of us doesn't have to suffer."

Oh, God. She didn't want them suffering. Her heart nearly broke at the thought. Should she tell them she was in love with both of them? How would they react?

She shook her head. She was fucked. Utterly, completely, totally fucked. What to do?

"I'll tell you what," she said. "If you're really serious about this—"

"Oh, we're serious, honey," Jon said.

"Okay. Then I'll spend an evening with each of you. Go out on a date, stay in, whatever you want to do. Tomorrow's Friday. We could start then."

That was the only way. Maybe she'd realize she loved one of them more than the other. Someone would get left out in the cold, but what could she do? Either that or reject them both, and then all three of them would be miserable.

"That work for you, Bri?" Jon asked.

The other man nodded. "Sure. So who's first?"

Jon pulled some loose change out of his pocket. "We flip a coin."

"How original," Eve said.

"Hey, it works." Brian smiled and turned to Jon. "Heads I win, tails you lose."

"Ha-ha." Jon flipped a quarter in the air. "Call it."

"Heads," Brian said.

Jon caught the coin and flipped it over to the back of his hand. "Heads it is." He showed them both the results. "Tomorrow night, honey, you're with Bri. The night after, it's my turn."

Eve plunked her elbows on the table and cupped her head in her hands. At the same time, her nipples ached and her pussy throbbed. What had she gotten herself into?

CHAPTER TWO

Eve inhaled the spicy scent of tomato, garlic, and basil as Brian set the table with the Italian takeout he'd brought home.

"So where'd Jon go off to tonight?" she asked.

"Don't know. But he agreed to give us the night. And I'm leaving tomorrow." He smiled, and his emerald eyes sparkled.

Her heart skipped. "Yeah? Where are you going?"

"I'm staying at Anna's."

"Oh." Jealousy speared Eve like a knife.

Brian and Anna, his best piano student, were friends, nothing more. Of course, two days ago, Eve and Brian had been only friends. Anna was blond and lithe—supermodel gorgeous—and a gifted pianist to boot.

His lips curled into a saucy grin. "That bother you?"

Eve's cheeks warmed. "Of course not."

"Good, because it's not like that with Anna and me. I love you, Eve. No one else."

The warmth in her cheeks turned to flame. She wanted to return his sentiment. Looking at him, basking in his kind affection, she knew she loved him. Could love only him. Could find true happiness with him alone.

Yet if Jon were there she'd be thinking the same thoughts. She'd been down this road before and it always led to the same place. She was perfectly happy and in love with Brian when they were alone. And she was perfectly happy and in love with Jon when they were alone. What the hell was the matter with her?

"Smells good," she said.

"I know you love Italian. This is from a little place I discovered a few weeks ago. I've been meaning to take you there."

"Why didn't we go tonight?"

"Because I want to be alone with you tonight, sweetheart." He finished setting out the food and uncorked a bottle of Chianti Classico. "Bruschetta. Penne arrabiata. Veal piccata. And dark chocolate gelato for dessert. I hope you like it."

All her favorites. How well he knew her. "It's lovely, Bri. Thank you."

Brian poured two glasses of Chianti, handed one to Eve, and clinked his glass to hers. "To tonight."

She smiled. "To tonight." The peppery wine warmed her mouth.

As she licked her lips, Brian took her glass from her and set it on the table next to his own. With slow, deliberate care, he cupped her cheek and lowered his lips to hers.

Their mouths melded together in a numbing kiss. A promise of more to come. He nibbled across her upper lip, tongued the corner of her mouth. Brian didn't tease. He dived in and took. Her blood boiled and she parted her lips. He plunged his tongue inside and wrapped it around hers. Her knees gave out. Strong arms coiled around her, steadied her.

She let out a soft sigh. Her first kiss with Brian. It was so much better than she'd ever imagined. He swept into her mouth and ravaged her as though he were pounding out a concerto on the piano. She'd often wondered whether Brian's kisses would be *piano* or *forte*.

Forte. Oh, so *forte*.

His full pink lips clamped around her tongue and sucked it deep. Open-mouthed and wet, the kiss was urgent, provocative. When he ripped his mouth from hers and nibbled on her neck, she inhaled a much needed breath.

"How do you think I like to fuck, Eve?" he whispered against her ear. "Do you think I like it slow and gentle?"

She shuddered and shook her head. His kiss had told the tale. "Fast, Bri. You like to fuck hard and fast."

"Hard and fast, sweetheart. I want to sink my cock into your pussy hard and fast."

"God." Eve trembled against Brian's muscled way too-clothed body. "Our dinner..."

He brushed his lips against her cheek. "Our dinner. I'm going to feed you, baby. And I want you to think about that kiss. And about that hard, fast fuck." He nipped her earlobe.

An inferno raged in her body. She'd think of nothing else. When he let her go and held out her chair for her, she sat quickly and took a long gulp of her Chianti. The clatter of dinner plates chimed in her ears as Brian fumbled in the kitchen.

In a few minutes, he returned with three dishes. He set a plate of pasta in front of her and a plate of toasted Italian bread and tomato bruschetta between them. He sat down, not across from her, but next to her. She locked her gaze on his musician's hands as he spread some of the tomato, basil, and garlic mixture atop a slice of bread. She inhaled the fresh fragrance. "Mmm."

"I know you love your bruschetta, sweetheart." He held it out to her. "Here. Take a bite."

The piquant flavors exploded across her tongue. "Jeez, Bri, that's fantastic." She licked her lips.

"Good?"

"The best."

"Mmm. Let me try." He leaned forward and licked the corner of her mouth.

God, she was on fire again. How was she going to get through this evening without fucking him silly? Had to be fair. Fair to Jon. If she fucked Bri, she'd have to... Oh God...

Distraction. She needed a distraction. She cleared her throat and prepared another piece of bruschetta. "Here, Bri."

She held it out to him and he took a large bite, chewed and licked his lips. Her heart pounded. How did he manage to make eating look sexy as hell?

"It's great," he said. "Though I preferred to eat it off you."

Heat slid to her pussy. The smoky aroma of roasted tomatoes and peppers in the arrabiata sauce tickled her nose. Spicy Italian cuisine and spicy hot man? A delicious combination. Brian poked his fork into the penne arrabiata and held it to Eve. She swallowed, letting the zesty flavor coat her tongue and throat.

"You eat like you dance." Brian winked. "You give it your all. You savor each taste and texture. I love to watch you eat. Just like I love to watch you dance."

Her cheeks warmed. "I'm thinking about opening a dance school." Shit, she was babbling. "I could open a small studio and teach part-time for now. Then full-time after I'm done performing."

"Done performing? What are you talking about?"

"Performers grow old quickly, you know. I've probably only got ten good years left as a dancer."

"Old? You're twenty-five, Eve. You light the world on fire with every shimmy, every flutter. Don't ever stop dancing."

She laughed. "No one wants to watch an old lady shake her booty."

"You think thirty-five will be old?"

"In the dance world, yeah, thirty-five is old. That's when dancers start to get face lifts and tummy tucks. Frankly, I don't want to do any of that."

He smiled his gorgeous smile. "You have the sexiest belly I've ever seen, sweetheart. But then, you already know how I feel about your belly. About all of you."

She let out her breath in a whoosh and shook her head. "I can't believe it."

"Believe what?" "This. All of this. That you love me. That Jon loves me."

Brian tensed at the mention of Jon. Just slightly, but Eve noticed the cords in his neck tighten. Eve noticed everything about Brian.

"Tell me something." He took a sip of wine. "What do you love about dancing?"

"You know why I dance, Bri. We've talked about it a million times. The same reason you play. We're artists. The dance calls to me."

"You're right." He took a bite of pasta and swallowed. "I guess what I really want to know is"—he hedged a little—"do you ever dance for...me?"

Her nipples burned through her bra. Did she dance for him? Only all the time. "Yeah. I dance for you." And for Jon, but that was better kept to herself right now. "Every time, Brian."

His eyes simmered. "That's why I play piano, did you know that? I play for you. You're in every note, every melody." He brushed her bottom lip with the pad of his thumb. "Every beat of every rhythm." He traced her jawline with sensual precision. "And every beat of my heart."

Chills skittered across her skin. Her heart thundered.

"Brian, that's the sweetest, most tender thing anyone's ever said to me."

"I love you, Eve. I knew it was wrong. I knew our agreement. But I can't help it. I see you every day. I watch how you take care of Jonny and me. And this place. You give your all to us, just like you give your all to dancing." He chuckled and dropped his gaze to her plate of pasta. "To eating." He cupped her cheeks with both hands. "How could I not fall in love with you?"

Her insides turned to mush, and a pang of longing shot through her. She loved this man so fucking much. "Oh, Brian."

He pulled her face to his in a crushing kiss. His tongue plunged into her mouth, swept over every crevice. It was a forceful, demanding kiss. A kiss from a man who knew exactly what he wanted.

Her. He wanted her. And God help her, she wanted him. Wanted to fuck him hard. Fuck him fast. Fuck him all night long. She summoned every last drop of strength she possessed and ripped her mouth from his. "The rest of our dinner—"

"Can wait." He drew a ragged breath. "Do you want me, Eve? Do you want to make love with me?"

Heavens, yes. More than she wanted to breathe. She nodded, her lips too numb to form the word.

"I want to play for you."

She nodded again. Lips still weren't working.

"Then will you dance for me? Dance for me, and then fuck me? Ride my cock and flutter your belly while I suck on your sweet nipples?"

"My nipples..." They stabbed at the lace of her bra. Would he suck her nipples hard? Like he kissed?

"Yeah, your nipples, sweetheart. I dream about them. Did

you know that? I dream about kissing every inch of you. Of sucking your pussy, fucking you in the ass. Did you know I like to fuck a woman in the ass?"

"I...I..."

"You ever done that before, Eve?"

Her skin ignited. Tingles shot from her nerve endings to her cunt. "No, Bri. I haven't."

"Maybe you'll let me fuck you there someday." He trailed his fingers down her arm, to her hip, and cupped her mound through her jeans. "Are you wet right now?"

Sopping, most likely. Her nipples strained against her turquoise tank. She was certain they were poking Brian's chest like mini torpedoes.

"I thought about going slow with you." He pressed moist kisses to her bare shoulders. "You smell great. Just like cinnamon. Then I decided, this is my one shot. My one shot to show you who I am. What it would be like for you to be with me, sweetheart. I love you. And I want you to know me."

"Yes, Bri. I want to know you. I do."

He pulled away, but only slightly. Enough to glue his gaze to hers. "You have the most beautiful eyes, Evonna Costello."

"They're plain old gray."

"They're silver. Silver with dark blue flecks. I could drown in them. I dream of drowning in them."

"Bri..."

He cupped her face in his palms, scorching her cheeks. "Come to bed with me?"

Her legs shook, and her pussy quivered. She nodded. She had to. She'd become a slave to his desires at some point. A willing slave, and she wanted this as much as he did.

Brian took her hand. Anticipation rocked through Eve.

She was really going to do it. She was going to sleep with Brian. Beautiful, artistic Brian. Perhaps he was the one. They had much in common, both being artists. Brian had always been so gentlemanly, well-mannered. But his kiss had been anything but gentle. Primal, urgent, full of raw power. *Forte*. His fucking would be the same.

Oh, to be fucked hard and fast. Her pussy pulsed. She hadn't been thoroughly fucked in months. He led her not to his bedroom, though, but to the front room, which housed his baby grand piano, a television, and a sofa. Nothing more fit with the large instrument. Eve did her own rehearsing at a nearby dance studio where she rented space.

"I-I thought you wanted to go to bed."

"Mmm, I do. More than you know. But remember? I want to play for you. And I want you to dance for me."

"There isn't room in here. Besides, you've seen me dance thousands of times."

He grinned. "Not naked."

Her nipples hardened to marbles. Naked? The thought had possibilities. His fingers brushed over her shoulder, down her arm, lighting sparks that catapulted to her core. His hands trailed up her back and expertly unclasped her bra through the cotton of her tank. She sucked in a breath as he lifted her tank and bra off in one graceful motion.

His gaze burned into her breasts. "Beautiful, sweetheart, just like I knew you'd be." He cupped her full mounds and thumbed her erect nipples. "I'm so hard right now, Eve. So hard for you."

Ripples of desire washed through her. She arched into his hands. He pinched her nipples, twisted them. Hard, just as she knew he would. So fucking good.

"God, Bri."

"You like that, baby?"

She nodded and her heart pounded.

"Perfect nipples. Perfect breasts."

"I-I thought Jon was the boob man." She gasped. "Oh!"

Brian's fingers tensed on her flesh for a moment, and then he relaxed. "It's okay. Just don't mention him again."

Regret swept through her. She didn't want to hurt Brian. "I'm sorry. This is your night."

He lowered his head. "I hope, in the end, all the nights with you will be mine." He clamped his firm lips around one nipple and tugged.

Forte. So good. Brian charged right in and seized what he wanted. Not gentle. Never gentle. Hard. Intense. Ferocious.

As he sucked, Eve was vaguely aware of him working the snap and zipper of her jeans. When the fabric slid down her hips, her thighs, below her knees, she kicked off her clogs and stepped out of her clothes. She stood, completely nude, a gorgeous man kissing her nipples, biting them, sending coils of raw energy to her throbbing pussy. Moisture coated her inner thighs.

As if he'd read her mind, he slid one hand across the slope of her breast, down her waist, over her hips, and slipped two fingers into her slick folds. He released her nipple. "Sweet God, you're wet, Eve." He pinched her labia together, massaged her clit. "I want to fuck you so bad right now."

She understood his need. She shared it. But he'd asked her to dance, and dance she would. "That feels so good, Bri. D-Do you still want to play? For me to dance?"

"Mmm, I sure do. I want you to dance for me. Only for me. Naked. Lots of flutters, baby."

"But first you'll play for me?"

He didn't smile. Simply gripped her shoulders and gazed at her with fiery eyes. "I always play for you, Eve." He said no more as he, still fully clothed, his jeans bulging at the crotch, took his seat on the black lacquered piano bench. His slender fingers stretched across the keys, and music drifted into the room. A lazy melody.

Eve sat next to him, the bench cool on her bare ass. Yet she was warm. So warm. The solid heat of Brian next to her consumed her. She laid her head on his shoulder and closed her eyes. The music wafted around her, and she breathed deeply. His musky male scent shimmered into her.

"I love your music, Bri."

"I love *you*," he murmured. "Dance for me?"

She nodded against his hard muscle and then rose from the bench. He launched into a slow Arabic tune. So he wanted slow. She could do slow. The small area she had to work with would lend itself well to slow.

She closed her eyes, let the rhythm saturate her. Her hips glided into figure eights. When she was one with the music, she opened her eyes. Brian didn't watch the keys. His smoldering gaze rested on Eve, and she slid into a full body undulation, her muscles responding to the notes. She swayed, swept up her long chestnut locks, and gyrated her hips in slow spirals. She released her hair and bowed forward, sweeping her body in an arc before she stood tall again and circled her chest. Her nipples poked forward, begging for attention, and without thinking she slid her hands around the rosy flesh of her breasts, cupped them, and plucked the two hard nubs.

"God, baby." Brian's playing never faltered as he watched, groaned.

Eve smiled to her audience of one. One of the only two who had ever mattered. She jiggled her legs to produce a hip shimmy and then, with a wink, she tensed her diaphragm and gave him a flutter.

The movement required a lot of power, a lot of energy, but Brian was worth it. She fluttered and fluttered, stopping and taking a breath as necessary, her body heating further. Need. Raw, aching need. As the muscles moved rapidly, she glided one hand over her belly to her triangle of mahogany curls and dipped a finger into her own juices.

"Damn, Eve." The music stopped and Brian rose abruptly. He removed his shirt.

Oh, his chest was beautiful. Eve had seen it many times before, but right now, in this moment, with her body on fire from the dance and her mind swirling with memories of his kisses, that chest was a sculpture from heaven itself. Wisps of reddish-brown hair scattered across the muscles. His nipples, turgid and copper, begged for her touch. His stomach was sleek and ripped, and as he unsnapped and unzipped his jeans, she riveted her gaze to what was about to be revealed.

His cock didn't disappoint. Massive and golden, it sprang from auburn curls. Brian kicked off his shoes and jeans and stood before her—fair and beautiful and clearly very turned on. He turned, fumbled in the pocket of his pants, and produced a condom. Within a few seconds he was sheathed.

"The piano, Eve." His voice was throaty and demanding. "Get on the fucking piano."

He didn't wait for her to move. He lifted her in strong sinewy arms and set her on the keyboard. Discordant notes rang in the air as her bottom sank onto the cool ivory keys.

"I'm going to fuck you like this," he said, spreading her

legs and positioning himself between them. "On the piano. God, I've dreamed of this so many times. Of taking you like this. Right here." He slammed his cock into her wet pussy.

The sigh that left her lips permeated the room. He filled a void, an aching void that had been empty far too long. His thrusts were vigorous. Unyielding. With each plunge, he touched more than the depths of her pussy. He probed the center of her heart, her soul.

"Ah, sweetheart. You're so tight." He drove into her deeper.

Bass notes clanged and vibrated as he pounded her, inharmonious and jarring, yet somehow in tune with his possession of her.

"So fucking tight and wet. You feel so good."

The sheer joy of being so thoroughly taken saturated every cell of Eve's body. A blaze kindled in her pussy, pulsed and radiated outward, erupting in tiny tingles across her flesh.

"Do you like it hard, Eve?" He leaned toward her, his breath a hot caress. "Do you like to be fucked this way?"

Her moan was her answer. Brian entwined his fingers in her curls and found her clit. He pinched the inflamed button, and she shattered. The climax raged inside her pussy. She spasmed around his cock. Her outer lips prickled, and tiny convulsions spread through her tummy, up to the rapid pounding of her heart, out to her arms and legs. Upward she soared until she floated above the piano.

Brian still hammered into her. She cried his name, begged him for more, and he gave it. He fucked her hard and fast, just like he'd promised. And just as she peaked, he thrust into her one last time and his release pulsated within her.

She lay atop the piano sated, her lover clamped between her legs, still inside her. She sighed. "Good, Bri."

He let out a husky chuckle. "Good doesn't even begin to describe it."

She smiled. "You aren't what I expected."

He winked. "You expected a nice gentlemanly fuck, didn't you?"

"Well, I'm not sure. Maybe, to a certain extent. I knew sex with you would be good, no matter what type it was."

"Good?" He curved his lips into a lazy half-grin. "Just good?"

"Okay, great."

"Hmm. Great. Not bad for the first round." He pulled away from her, disposed of the condom, and extended his hand to help her off the piano. "We're by no means done, sweetheart."

Eve's breath caught. Not done? Thank God. She didn't want to be done. She let out a nervous laugh. "I'm yours for the night."

"And the night is still young." He kissed her fingertips. Back to gentlemanly.

Her insides squirmed. How she loved him!

"I hope our dinner isn't too cold," she said.

"That's what the microwave is for." He pulled her into his embrace.

Perspiration dripped between them. Eve inhaled the crisp male scent of Brian. So good.

"What do you want to do, then?"

He cupped one swollen breast and pressed his lips to her cheek. "I want to finish our dinner."

"Okay."

"And then I want to eat you for dessert."

CHAPTER THREE

Eve was as tight as he'd imagined. Brian sat across from her, both of them still naked. Her sexy nipples drew his gaze. He'd watched her gray eyes twinkle as she ate, listened to her gush about the food. Had seen her face light with joy as she talked about her dancing, his music. Their goals.

They discussed the small studio she wanted to open. Even considered sharing a studio, where he could teach piano, rather than having his students come to the loft. She'd be a great teacher. She'd give it her all, as she did with everything else. Just like he gave his music. Just like Jonny gave to his clients.

Shit. His body cramped a little at the thought of his friend. His best friend. Also his competition. Competition for the woman he loved more than life itself.

"You okay, Bri?"

As usual, her perception amazed him. She always knew when something was bothering him.

He inhaled, let his breath out in a slow stream, and reached for Eve's hand. "I'm good. Better than good, in fact. I'm so happy to be here with you tonight."

"Oh, Bri..." Her voice deepened. "You're so sweet. And the lovemaking... Wow."

He kissed her fingertips. She had beautiful hands, his Eve. "Wow is right." He smiled into her incredible eyes. Mesmerizing. He could lose himself in her eyes, in her soft, tight body. "You ready for dessert?"

"Dark chocolate gelato? Are you kidding? You bet I'm ready."

Brian rose and took her hand. "I was thinking we'd save that for later. I had something much sweeter in mind."

"Oh..." She reddened again, from her cheeks, down her neck, across the gorgeous flesh of her breasts.

His cock turned to stone. "Come with me." He led her to his bedroom.

"Bri..."

"Lie down, baby, and spread your legs."

"It's been...so long since anyone's..."

He groaned. "I'll try not to disappoint you."

"God, you couldn't."

He kissed her lips, her neck. Damn, she smelled good, tasted even better. He tongued one nipple, and then the other. Such a smooth, sweet texture. The buds pebbled against his tongue. He kissed downward, over her taut belly. So sexy. He dipped his tongue into her navel and she giggled. Ah-ha. A tickle spot. Good to know.

Then he eased farther down, buried his nose in her springy chestnut curls, and inhaled her musky bouquet. Mmm, she was going to be a fucking feast. He dipped his tongue onto her clit, and she quivered beneath him, sighing.

"Oh, Bri..."

He loved her voice. Loved her saying his name. Loved being here with her. He slid his tongue between her dripping pussy lips. Her honey was sweet and tart at the same time. Delicious, as he'd always known she'd be. Delicious, because he loved her.

"Bri, I love to be licked. Did you know that?"

"Mmm." He inhaled and gave her cunt a wet kiss. "I'll lick

you anytime you want, baby."

He forced his tongue into her, and her thighs clamped around him. Her pussy pulsed beneath his lips. She was near climax already. His cock twitched. Her smooth, silky labia caressed his tongue. He sucked them between his teeth, nibbled them, tugged on them. Damn, she had one gorgeous pussy. Her moans and sighs fueled his lust. He dived deeper into her channel, plundered her with lips, teeth, and tongue. He wanted to make her come. Wanted to suck all the cream out of her until she was begging for his cock in her pussy, her mouth, her ass.

"Bri, that's so good!"

Her breathless gasp stoked the fire already blazing within him. He sucked on her clit, nipped it, and plunged two fingers into her tight sheath. Her pussy clamped down on him. The spasms started slowly, and then accelerated, gaining strength, urgency.

"Brian, my God!"

he arched toward him, hugging his head with her creamy thighs, grinding that sweet, wet pussy into his lips. He released her clit, raised his head to watch her face. A luminous coating of perspiration covered her. Her burning eyes locked onto his.

"Yeah, sweetheart. Come. Come for me."

The convulsions continued around his fingers. He swirled them in circles and massaged her G-spot. Her tiny puckered hole beckoned him, and he lubricated her with her own cream and massaged her anus, waiting for her to object.

She didn't. Slowly, gently, he breached the tight entrance with the tip of his third finger. She shattered again. Fresh nectar coated his hand. He latched onto her clit and sucked her delicious essence. Her spasms increased.

"Bri!"

"You like that?" He plunged deeper. "You like my finger in your tight little ass?"

"Yes. God, yes!" Her thighs tensed around him. She grabbed fistfuls of his hair and forced his face to meld to her flesh.

Still he fingered her in both places. And still, she came. Her pussy pulsed and pulsed.

The longest damn orgasm he'd ever given a woman. His heart rejoiced that he'd given it to Eve.

When her body relaxed, he slipped his fingers from her pussy and ass, gave her cunt lips a wet kiss, climbed upward, and clamped his mouth to hers. She wove her arms around his neck and invaded him with her sweet tongue. The kiss was harsh, frenzied. Full of passion and emotion. He threw himself into the meeting of their mouths. Into her. Like a wolf declaring his mate, he bit at her tongue. Sucked on it. Growled as he slurped her bottom lip between his teeth.

Mine. Damn it Eve, you're mine.

His cock nudged against her slick entrance. Couldn't fuck her yet. Hadn't put on a condom. Damn. Still he humped against her, fought the urge to thrust inside. Rubbed his arousal against the curly hairs covering her mound. He was about to burst.

He ripped his mouth from hers and turned onto his back, his arm strewn across his forehead and eyes.

"Bri?" Eve's voice was edgy. "Something wrong?"

"No, baby. No. It's just...I want to fuck you so bad. Pound into you. Right now. But I don't have a condom on. I had to move away or I would have taken you."

She smiled at him, her eyes sparkling. "We can remedy

that situation, you know. Where do you keep them?"

"Nightstand drawer." Sweat dripped from his forehead. His cock stood rigid, wanting.

In a few seconds, warm fingers enwrapped him, sheathed him. What he wouldn't give to fuck her without the rubber. But that would have to wait.

She climbed on top of him and eased onto his cock. Sweet, sweet suction. Damn, she was tight as a virgin.

"Ah..."

Her sigh drifted over his chest like a soft summer breeze.

"Let me take care of you, Brian," she said. She began to ride him slowly, and then she ground down, taking his entire length.

He fought the urge to take control, to thrust upward into her and fuck her fast again.

"Watch me," she said. "Watch me dance for you."

He opened his eyes and caught the flutter. As she rode him, her belly rippled, and God damn it, every one of those sexy muscle contractions tightened her hold on his cock. Her breasts jiggled gently against her chest, and her red nipples, hard and tight, poked outward, as though looking for a mouth to suck on them.

"You're beautiful." He stopped to take a breath. "So gorgeous, sweetheart. That's it. Dance for me."

His cock threatened to explode. One more flutter, and...

He grabbed her hips and thrust upward. Her cunt drummed around him. She moaned his name, moaned how good he was, how hot he made her. He tensed, holding off.

Oh, he wanted to come. Wanted to release into that gorgeous sweet pussy of hers. And he would. But not yet.

He pulled her down to his mouth for a long, deep kiss.

When she broke the kiss, her warm breath caressed his cheek. "That was amazing, Bri."

He smiled. "My pleasure."

"Tell me. What would you like? I want to please you. Make you feel as good as you made me feel. I'll do whatever you want. A blowjob? You want to fuck again? Just tell me."

He groaned. Either one would be heaven on earth. But would she give him what he longed for most? He hesitated only for a moment then met her gaze. This was his one chance. She had to know him. All of him. He had to be honest, even if it meant she might reject him.

"I like to be in control in the bedroom, Eve. I like it hard. I like it fast. I like to take a woman. I mean, really take her."

"I know that. I love it. Really."

"Will you give me something?"

"Anything you want."

"I want to fuck your ass, sweetheart. I want to make love to you that way."

"Oh..."

"It's up to you. But that's what I like."

"Will it...hurt?"

He caressed her soft cheek and wiped away a drip of slick perspiration. "I won't let it hurt, baby. I'll get you ready. And if you're not ready to take it that far, I'd love for you to suck my cock and I'll pound your pussy again."

"I want to please you."

"You do, Eve. Never doubt that."

"I'm just not sure." "Listen"—he took her hand, kissed her fingertips—"anal sex takes a lot of trust. I want you to trust me, Eve. Trust that I'll make it good for you, that I'll take care of you. But if you can't yet, I understand."

"Bri, I know you'd never hurt me."

"So you trust me?"

"Of course I do."

"Then?" He tensed, on edge. Would she let him take her ass? The thought had him near climax already.

She cupped his cheek. "Your stubble feels nice."

He chuckled. "Thanks. I think."

"You're so handsome. I love your hair." She toyed with it, let it slip through her fingers. "Your face is something out of a Renaissance painting. Beautiful. Classic."

"I think you're beautiful too, sweetheart. But you already know that."

"You're beautiful on the inside too, Bri."

"So are you, and that's more important."

She smiled that dazzling smile. "You're right. It is more important. And that's why I trust you, Brian. I trust you not to hurt me. I want to please you. So my answer is yes. I'd like for you to make love to me the way you want to. The way that pleases you. And that will please me."

His insides melted. "Sweetheart, I love you so much." What he wouldn't give to hear her say those words back. "Are you sure?"

"Very."

His cock threatened to explode. He donned a new condom, gave Eve a deep openmouthed kiss, and turned her onto her tummy. "I'm going to massage you a little. Some people use anal plugs. I prefer to use what I have." He kissed her sleek shoulder. "My fingers and my tongue."

She shuddered against him. "Okay."

He rained kisses down her back, across her rosy butt cheeks, and slid his tongue into the crease between them. Salty from sweat, her rosy hole puckered under his tongue. Mmm, nice. His cock throbbed. He inhaled deeply. God he wanted to take her now. Make her his the way he longed to. But he had to wait. Had to get her ready before he pounded into that virginal flesh.

He traced tiny circles around her anus with his tongue. Her fragrant musk teased his taste buds. Gradually, her muscles relaxed against him and he probed her, just a touch. She let out a soft sigh.

"Good, sweetheart?"

"Yeah. Good. I like it so far."

"You're going to love it, I promise." He nibbled at her fleshy butt cheeks. Damn, she had a gorgeous ass. Perfect.

He reached into his nightstand for a tube of lubricant, squeezed the cool gel onto his fingers, and rubbed it between her cheeks.

"Oh, cold!"

"It'll warm up, baby. Relax."

"Mmm." She closed her eyes. Her dark lashes rested against her rosy cheeks. So beautiful.

He massaged her anus with the lubricant and slowly inserted one finger. "Relax," he said again. "Just go with it."

Her breathing stayed steady and he probed another half-inch, and then another.

"Good, baby?"

"Yeah. It's good."

He smiled. He was pleasing the woman he loved, sharing his whole self with her. He gently added another finger. The ring of muscle tensed—just a little but he noticed. "Breathe, sweetheart. That's it."

As she loosened, he fingered her deeper, massaging the

band of muscle. She was smooth inside and so tight. She was going to be a sweet, sweet fuck.

"Oh, Brian." Her voice thickened. "That feels so good."

"That's what I want, sweetheart. I want you to feel good." He penetrated farther until he was knuckle-deep, fucking her with two fingers.

Eve slid her knees forward and thrust her ass in the air. She was ready. God, so was he. "You want me, baby? You want my cock?"

"Oh Bri, yeah."

His whole body shook as he withdrew his fingers and positioned his cock at her puckered entrance. Desire pulsed through his stiff flesh. He slowly pushed his cock head past the tight band of muscle.

She gasped.

"It's okay, baby. That's the toughest part. Trust me."

"I trust you. I want this."

He eased in. Sweet ass, so tight. Her hot tunnel gripped him, embraced him. He took another inch, and then another, until he was buried balls-deep in her heat.

"Full, Bri. I'm so full."

"I want to fill you, baby. Let me know when you're ready for me to fuck you. God, I want to fuck you so bad. I want to hammer your ass, Eve."

She was so damn tight! He could blow right now.

"Now." Her hips shimmied backward against him. "Fuck me now."

Slowly he pulled out and thrust back in. Damn, he'd really have to focus to keep from coming.

"Fast, Bri." She wiggled. "I thought you liked it hard and fast."

Was she serious? Saints be praised! That luscious body tempted him beyond control. But as much as he desired to pound her, she wasn't ready for hard and fast anal, no matter how turned on she was.

"I do, Eve. But I want to take it slow right now. I want to savor you." He grasped her hips and pressed into her slowly and gently.

Her tight muscles clenched around his cock. Sweet, hot possession. Again he plunged balls-deep, and then again. When he knew he couldn't hold off any longer, he reached in front of her, slapped her wet pussy a few times with his fingers, and plucked at her swollen clit.

When she bucked in climax, his cock throbbed, but he held himself steady. More. He wanted more. He'd make her come again and again. When her spasms slowed, he dipped one finger into her pussy and rubbed the juice over her sensitive clit.

"Come again," he commanded.

"I can't..." She panted against the cotton sheets. "I've come so many times already, Bri. I just...can't"

"You can, baby. Relax." He swirled around her clit, worked her slowly at first, and then increased the pressure. All the while his cock was buried in her tight ass. "Come on, sweetheart." He pulled out and slowly eased back in. His cock twitched.

No, not yet.

Her body went limp, her lips trembled against the pillow that cradled her head. "I...I can't."

"Oh, you can. And you will." He withdrew his fingers and wrapped his arms around her soft belly, pulling her against him.

Ah, her skin—so soft and sensual. Again his cock threatened to release. He clenched his teeth, forcing back his climax.

"You'll come until I tell you not to, sweetheart." He pulled out to the tip, and then plunged into her again. He leaned down and rained tiny kisses across her glistening shoulders as he fingered her clit again.

As she exploded, he thrust two fingers into her warm, wet pussy and let her convulsions hug his hand. God damn, she was hot.

"Bri! I'm coming!" She collapsed.

He pulled her to him. Their perspiration mingled as their bodies slid together. He inhaled her musky sweetness. She smelled of cinnamon and sex. Of love. His love.

He finally let himself go. Tiny vibrations began in his balls and swam along the base of his cock. The tremors amplified until he spilled his seed in spasms that rippled through his entire body.

"Eve!" His shout was hoarse, raspy. "Eve, I love you." He thrust once more into her body and gave her everything he had. He hoped it was enough.

She lay panting beneath him, her body glowing with mist. He withdrew, disposed of the condom and lay down next to her.

"I love you," he whispered.

She didn't return the words. He didn't expect her to.

But she crawled into his arms. She kissed his lips, his neck, his chest. She sucked on a nipple. "Mmm," she said. "You taste good."

His cock twitched. He was ready for her again. His balls ached already. This was going to be one long, good night.

CHAPTER FOUR

"So what do you want to do tonight?"

Jon's question stunned Eve. What did she want to do? Brian hadn't asked what she'd wanted to do. He'd taken charge of the food, the sex, everything. He certainly hadn't forced her into any of it, but he'd definitely been in control. She'd assumed Jon would do the same.

Now, as they stood outside the studio where she'd just finished showering after a strenuous practice, he was asking her what she wanted and she had no idea how to respond. "Whatever you want, Jon. I want to get to know you, like I did Bri."

"Did you and Bri sleep together?"

Her cheeks heated.

His deep chocolate eyes betrayed his feelings. A touch of sadness laced them. He shook his head slowly. "Forget I asked that. I don't want to know."

Eve smiled and took his hand. Those long thick fingers, warmly entwined around hers, never failed to turn her on. "Let's concentrate on tonight, okay? This is your night. So why don't you tell me what you'd like to do."

He grinned and his dimples lit up his dark-stubbled face. Man, he really was ruggedly gorgeous. So different from Brian, who was male-model handsome in a refined way. Jon's onyx hair fell to his shoulders in tousled waves, as though he'd just gotten out of bed. He always sported a few days growth of beard, and those firm, full red lips, those thick fingers...ideal fodder for fantasy.

"I'd like to make love to you all night, honey, but I've wanted that for about a year now."

A year? He'd had feelings for her for a whole year? She hadn't thought to ask Brian how long he'd been in love with her.

Her own feelings for both of them had developed slowly. Indeed, she hadn't recognized them for what they were until a few months ago. She'd dated many men, all nice guys, but her belly never tumbled the way it did when she was at home with Jon and Brian. Something as simple as watching a movie together got her going. Being with them was so easy. They each knew everything about the other two.

Her last boyfriend had been amazing—intelligent, funny, handsome—but sex with him hadn't moved her. Not the way she'd soared last night with Brian. When she'd found herself counting the moments until her date ended so she could get home to her guys, she realized her plight.

She was in love. Not with her boyfriend. With Jon and Brian.

They were wonderful men, good souls, and of course, extremely physically appealing. She'd fantasized about them for years. The love had come gradually. Now, inside her heart, they were both omnipresent. A part of her.

She smiled into Jon's dark gaze. "I might be able to accommodate you. But maybe we should eat first. What sounds good?"

"Well...there's this great new place that opened up next to the gym. It's gourmet food that's healthy."

"Healthy, huh?" Eve grimaced. "I don't know, Jonny."

He let out a laugh. "I know you're a good Italian girl who

likes her good Italian food, fat, carbs, and all. But healthy food can be delicious, I promise." He leaned down and kissed her cheek. "Let me show you."

He kissed her cheek again, leaving a spark where his lips had touched.

"Come on," he squeezed her hand, "we can walk from here."

She sighed. She wanted to experience a date with him, after all. She just hoped she didn't have to eat some kind of tofu burger. The last time Jon had cooked, she and Brian had sneaked out for pizza afterward.

"Ha, I know what you're thinking."

She smiled. "You do, huh?"

"Yeah. I do. I know every little look, every nuance on your beautiful face, Eve. Right now you're thinking about the food I try to make at home."

Amazing, how he could read her. Truth was, she could read both him and Brian just as well. "How did you know?"

He laughed and shook his head. "I admit I'm not much of a cook. But the chef at this new place is, I assure you. You won't be disappointed."

Hand in hand they walked the two blocks to the restaurant, talking about nothing in particular. Eve relished the warmth of Jon next to her. He was so big, so ruggedly beautiful. And those eyes... Though he wasn't as talkative as Brian, Jon said so much with his dark, blazing eyes.

As Eve perused the menu at The Zodiac, she was surprised that most of the choices sounded pretty good. "How's the Caesar salad?" she asked Jon.

"Good. The dressing is made with low fat yogurt and olive oil."

"Yum." Eve rolled her eyes.

"Don't knock it till you've tried it, honey."

When her Caesar salad arrived, complete with the anchovies she'd requested, Jon's face twisted into a grimace.

"How you can eat those is beyond me."

"You know I love 'em." Eve flashed a grin. "Don't knock 'em till you've tried 'em."

"I'll pass."

"If you really loved me, you'd taste one," she teased, holding out her fork.

"Hairy, smelly fish have nothing to do with love."

Eve let out a laugh before she took another bite. Banter was fun. They talked about Jon's job, about running his own business, and Eve picked his brain about the business side of the dance studio she wanted to open.

Jon possessed brains as well as brawn. He'd run a successful training business for three years now, and Eve soaked up ideas as they chatted and ate their meals. Her entrée was remarkably tasty.

"I can help you with your business plan," Jon said. "Have you thought about what your mission statement will be?"

What the hell was he talking about? "Mission statement?"

"Every successful business needs one. Mine is to educate, motivate, and support each client by way of an individualized program designed to maximize his physical and emotional health."

"Wow." Eve's fork stopped halfway to her mouth. "That's beautiful, Jonny. So thorough, yet so succinct."

"That's what makes a good mission statement." He smiled. "Have you forgotten I majored in business as well as physical education?"

She shook her head. She hadn't forgotten. She just hadn't given it a second thought since college five years ago.

"So what would be a good mission statement for my studio?"

"Only you can decide that," he said. "But I'll be happy to help."

Her mind churned. Why did she want to teach? Certainly not because she knew she'd have to give up performing eventually, though that was a consideration. Because she loved to dance. She was good at it, and she wanted to share her love with others. Be a mentor to students who could someday achieve, and hopefully surpass, her success.

"You're thinking," Jon said. "Your pretty lips are mushed together."

How did he do that? "Just considering my mission statement. There's so much I want to put in it."

He smiled, and her heart melted. Gorgeous didn't begin to describe this man.

"That's part of what I love about you, honey. Your tenacity. You'll be a wonderful dance teacher. You'll give it your all, just like you do every time you dance."

The warmth of a blush drifted over her flesh. "Thank you. That's a lovely compliment."

"It's the truth." Tiny sparks trickled over her. "Well, no more about mission statements. That's business. Tonight's for pleasure."

She patted her lips with her napkin. "I have to admit, this was a great meal, Jonny. I couldn't even tell that my eggplant parmesan was low fat."

"Told you." He scribbled on the check and handed it to the waitress. "Ready to go?"

"Yeah." Eve stood and gathered her purse. Her hand found his, and they walked the four blocks to their loft.

The delicate evening breeze brushed Eve's heated skin like a soft embrace. When they reached the door to the loft, Jon bent and kissed her cheek. His rough stubble scraped her smooth skin. Chills crept along her arms. He pulled her into his arms, his large muscled body pressing into her. His long arms circled her waist.

"I love you." His whisper caressed her neck. "I know you can't say it back, and I understand, but I've been dying to tell you for so long. I'll probably say it a hundred times tonight."

Heat pooled between her legs. She wanted to say it back. She did love him. But just last night she'd wanted to say the same words to Brian. Surely she was flawed. Some weird psychological disorder. She'd had many male companions over the years, yet had never fallen in love with any of them. Now, she found herself in love with two men.

Flawed. Definitely flawed.

"Honey? You look a little troubled."

Jon's words cut into her. Now was not the time to ruminate on her problem. She owed Jon a night, and she wanted it as much as he did. "Would you kiss me, Jon?"

He smiled a lazy half-smile. "You got it." He turned her in his arms and brushed those beautiful lips back and forth against hers.

Spine-tingling. That's what his kiss was. He traced her lips with his tongue. Teasing. Provoking. So different than Brian.

Nope. Not going to think about Brian.

She opened her lips, and Jon slid his tongue in. Hot, wet, delicious. He tasted of cinnamon and cream. Warm, comforting, yet intense at the same time. Delectable.

A soft groan hummed into her mouth. He was enjoying this. God, so was she. His velvety tongue tangled with hers. Weak-kneed and limp, she sighed into his inviting mouth, unprepared for the passion and magnitude of such a gentle kiss.

Because I love him. It's passionate and intense because I love him and he loves me.

He broke the kiss and drew a ragged breath. "Honey, I love you so much." He trailed moist kisses over her cheek to her lobe. He nibbled on it, traced the outer shell of her ear, and blew on the wetness.

She shivered.

"Will you dance for me?"

Warmth throbbed in her pussy. She nodded. "If you want me to. I always dance for you. You and Bri."

His arms tensed around her. "I don't want to talk about Bri tonight."

She nodded again. "I know. I'm sorry."

"It's okay. But this is my night."

"I understand." He smiled.

Emotion tugged at her tummy. His smile could melt steel.

"I want you to dance with veils. I love to watch you peel the veils away from your costume. It's so smooth, so beautiful, Eve, and no one does it like you."

"Let me guess." She arched her eyebrows and let out a giggle. "You want me to do it naked."

His full lips curved into a resplendent grin. "I hadn't thought of that. But I'm definitely in favor of the plan." He pushed the front door open.

Eve gasped. Their loft had morphed into an Arabian paradise. Colorful tapestries of purple, dark gold, midnight blue, and scarlet hung from the walls, and sheer silver veiling covered the lamps and created a gossamer glow. Ornate bottles sat on the end tables and piano, and Eve expected pink smoke to erupt into a genie at any moment. The dining table had been moved in front of the couch, and royal blue candles flamed on each corner. Incense burned next to one of the genie bottles, and Eve inhaled the exotic scent of jasmine. The soft strains of a violin haunted the newly adorned room. She turned to Jon, whose dark eyes were glowing.

"How?"

"I called Mac over at the Oasis. He sent a few guys over to decorate while we were at dinner."

"Oh..." She let out her breath in a sigh.

"You like it?" His large, muscled body pressed into her from behind, and his arms spiraled around her waist.

She clutched his warm hands and craned her neck to look up into his dark gaze. "I love it, Jonny. It's beautiful."

"Perfect for your dance, honey."

Eve's nipples pushed against her cotton blouse. "Okay. There's not much room here, but—"

"Who needs room? We have a perfectly good solid oak table."

"You want me to dance on the table?"

"Yeah, I sure do. You were meant for a stage."

"A table's hardly a stage, Jonny."

"A table's a great stage, and I'll have the best seat in the house."

"It won't hold my weight."

"Solid oak, Eve. I know how much you weigh. It'll be fine."

"Well, okay. If it's what you want."

"It's what I want. I love to watch you dance."

"Give me a few minutes." Eve rushed to her bedroom and stripped naked.

Naked. Jon was going to see her naked. A glance in her full-length mirror showed the rosy blush she already knew was blanketing her body. Oh, yes, she wanted him to see her naked. Just as she'd wanted Brian to see her naked.

She grabbed three veils—sheer red, sheer black, and sparkling silver—draped them around her body, and returned to the kitchen where Jon had cleared the table.

His gaze met hers, and his face reddened. "God, honey, I can see your breasts through that silver veil. They're as gorgeous as I knew they'd be. Your nipples are red. Fuck, they're red."

Tingles raced over Eve's skin. Her body shook. How could she dance like this?

Oh, she could. She would. For Jon.

A slow acoustic melody drifted around her. Jon had chosen perfect music for a veil dance. She stepped onto a chair and then onto the table. The diaphanous fabric titillated her bare nipples. They hardened even further into stony nubs. She twirled around and lifted her arms above her head, forming the veils into three spirals that circled her nude body. Ripples, in time with the soft drum beat under the melody, threaded through her pussy. She stopped the turn, regained her balance by focusing on an audience member.

Jon. His eyes smoldered. Her body blazed. Her cunt throbbed. She made love to Jon with this dance. It was for him. Only for him tonight. In one smooth movement, she swirled the veils behind her and held them with arms outstretched, a curtain behind her nude body. Slowly she circled her hips, and then her chest, the veils a gauzy backdrop for her performance.

Oh, she'd danced with veils thousands of times. But never naked and never for Jon alone.

The veil dance was one of the most sensual dances a belly dancer performed, second perhaps only to floor work, which Eve didn't do. The veils became part of the dancer, an extension, and they did so for Eve now.

She leaned forward, swept them over Jon's head, engaged him, and wrapped them around her body once more. Once covered in the sheer material, she shimmied her shoulders. Jon's favorite move, because it highlighted her ample breasts. Now unclothed, they jiggled, and her nipples poked through the veil.

Jon's groan resounded above the music. "Come here, honey. Come to me."

She swirled the veils over her head and released them. They drifted to the floor in a cascade of translucent color as she sat down on the edge of the table and faced Jon.

He pulled her onto his lap. The bulge in his jeans poked at her wet folds. "Do you know I could see your pussy, Eve? It was glistening." He let out a breath. "Gorgeous, pink, and glistening, damn it." He cupped her breasts and thumbed her hard nipples. "You're so beautiful. These are amazing." He pulled one forward and took the nipple into his mouth. "God," he said against a mouthful of flesh, "I've wanted to do this for so long."

Searing heat jolted through her. Those beautiful lips were lethal. She'd always known their power. He suckled her gently at first, little licks and kisses. His mouth on her was a luscious sight, and her pussy pulsed against his arousal. She ground into him and his denim-clad erection grazed her clit. When his teeth scraped her hard nipple, she thrust down onto him harder. She needed him. Needed his hard cock deep inside her.

"Jon." Her voice was a series of rapid pants. "I need you. Please."

He growled against her nipple, and the vibration buzzed through her. He stood, still holding her, and she clamped her legs around his waist. He kissed her hard and deep as he walked to his bedroom. Once there, he laid her gently on his rumpled bed.

"Tell me what you want, honey." He pulled his green polo shirt over his tousled waves, baring his sculpted chest. Dark hair scattered over golden muscle and sinew. Mountainous, magnificent.

"I want you, silly."

"I'll give it to you any way you want it."

"I want to know what you want, Jonny. This is your night, remember? Let me please you."

"I want you, Eve. In every way possible. I want to suck that pretty pink pussy of yours. I want your gorgeous lips wrapped around my cock." He fingered the snap of his jeans and popped it open.

As he readied to tackle his zipper, a cell phone jingled from the living room.

"Crap," Eve said.

"It's mine. I forgot to turn it off. Stay right there." Jon resnapped his jeans and left the room.

Eve lounged on the bed, buried her face in Jon's pillow, and inhaled. Vanilla male musk. Jon. Her pussy pulsed between her thighs. Here she was in the same boat as last night. So ripe she'd fall from the vine.

She reached between her legs and found her swollen nub. She dipped into her juices and swirled them over her clit, stimulating herself. Her skin heated and tingled, and she imagined Jon licking her, fucking her with his tongue. She was near climax when he returned.

"Sorry about that," he said.

Eve had no time to worry about who might have been calling Jon at this hour. Right now, she was so turned on she thought she might burst. She wanted his tongue, his beautiful full lips.

"Lick me, Jonny. Lick my pussy. I'm so close."

"God, Eve." His jeans still on, he lowered his head between her legs. He traced his tongue over the sensitive skin of one thigh then the other.

She sighed, and her skin tingled from the moist attack. When his tongue slid between her swollen cunt lips, she arched her hips. "Just like that. Yeah, baby. Suck me."

"Damn, you taste good, honey." His lips—those gorgeous lips—clamped onto her clit, but only for a second.

Such a tease! He sucked her labia into his mouth, and the slurping sounds raced through her. So good.

His voice murmured against her. "Pretty pussy. Sweet Eve. Mmm."

His sleek tongue probed her channel, slurped her inner lips, tantalized her. Her skin rippled, and she clamped her thighs around his head, urging him toward her clit. Still he teased her, tormented her.

"Jonny, please. You've got to let me come."

His chuckle vibrated into her slick folds, buzzed through her body. "Since you said the magic word..."

He plunged one of those wonderful thick fingers into her, and she imploded into fragments of vibrant color, a kaleidoscope of vivid images. Her pussy clamped onto Jon's finger and he continued sliding it in and out, massaging her, milking the last drops of climax from her.

"Oh Jonny, that was perfect. I always knew you had magic fingers."

"You thought about my fingers?"

"I thought about you a lot. You and Br— Oh God. Sorry."

"It's okay."

But it wasn't. She could tell by the hurt in his voice. She'd make it up to him. Big time. She sat up and unzipped his jeans. His cock was like the rest of him—majestic and magnificent. Huge. As long as Bri's, but thicker. One purple vein traveled around the top and disappeared underneath. A fucking work of art. She clamped her fingers around its girth.

"I want to suck that gorgeous cock, Jonny. I want to swallow you whole."

He groaned. "God. Please, honey."

She smiled into his blazing eyes, flicked her tongue, and lapped up the pearl of pre-cum that had emerged. Mmm, salty and male. She loved giving head. Loved being in control over a man like that. She circled her tongue over him and reveled in his moans and shudders. She licked the underside, swirled around his balls, sucked each one into her mouth, gently at first, and then harder. She nipped his muscled thighs and kissed his balls again. The soft dark hair covering them tickled her nose and cheeks. She inhaled. Pure male musk. Intoxicating.

"Eve, damn, that's good."

She grinned against his sac, caught her breath. She showered little kisses along his length and sucked just his cock head between her lips. All the while, lightning flashed to her pussy. She undulated her hips in time with the thrusts of her mouth on Jon's shaft. So much like the dance. Sensual, evocative. She plunged downward onto him and took his full length deep into her throat.

"God, Eve!"

She released him. "Good?"

"Amazing. Don't stop."

"Wouldn't think of it." She gave him what she hoped was a sexy grin and returned to his erection. Had it swelled bigger? Beautiful, just beautiful. She licked it all over, coating it with the sheen of her saliva. She loved the salty male taste of him. "I want you to come in my mouth, Jon."

He thrust upward, and his cock head grazed the back of her throat. "I can't, honey. Want to come...in you."

She gave his cock head a wet kiss. "There's lots of time for that. Please, baby. I want you to. Fuck my mouth and come in me."

"God." He thrust again.

She took him even deeper. The vibrations started at his base and tantalized her lips. They surged through his length, and his cream spilled down her throat in convulsive spurts and then slowed to a warm river. When he finished, she released him and licked her lips. Mmm, Jon.

"Aw, honey, that was amazing." He reached for her.

She crawled into his embrace. *I love you*. The words were on the tip of her tongue. How she longed to set them free. But she couldn't. Not yet. Not until she'd resolved the issue in her own mind. And right now she still loved Jon and Brian equally. They were so different, each unique. But she loved them both with an absolute passion.

She leaned over and gave Jon a deep, open-mouthed kiss. When she paused to take a breath, he pushed a few strands of moist hair behind her ear.

"You're beautiful."

"So are you, Jon." His smile speared her heart.

"Hungry? There's some dark chocolate gelato in the fridge. Dark chocolate's chock-full of antioxidants, you know."

She couldn't help a giggle. But she'd shared the gelato with Brian. She wasn't sure she could eat it with Jon. "I'm stuffed from that amazing meal."

"Too stuffed for chocolate? Who are you and what have you done with Eve Costello?"

She smiled at his joke. "I'm truly full, but I sure could go for a glass of water."

"You got it," he said, his eyes sparkling, "and then back to bed."

CHAPTER FIVE

Eve gulped down her glass of water, gazed at him, and smiled, her silver eyes sparkling. Jon's cock rose. A fine line creased her forehead. Only slightly, but he noticed.

"You're thinking again."

"Mmm. Thinking about how much I want to go back to bed with you."

"Works for me." He took her hand. "But first tell me something."

"Okay."

"I know you and Bri have a lot more in common than you and I do."

"Jonny, I thought you didn't want to talk about Bri."

"I don't. Except...well...I want to understand. I get that you're both artists. And you both talk about how the dance, or the music in Brian's case, calls to you."

"It's hard to explain any better than that."

He wanted to understand. Had a fierce need to get inside her head and learn every little essence that made her tick. "Try. Please."

"All right." She set the glass down on his nightstand. "I see dancing as a metaphor for life. Like moving through time and space, you know?"

"Yeah?" He didn't really get it, but oh, he wanted to.

"Yeah. Especially belly dancing. It's one of the most ancient forms of dance, and it's very empowering for women.

We use the parts of our bodies that are inherently female. We dance in bare feet to connect to the energy of the earth. And those flutters that Brian likes? They originated as a celebration of childbirth."

"Wow." He nodded as her words sank into his mind. He was getting it. He was getting her. And damn, he loved her all the more.

"And also, dance stimulates the physical, emotional, and spiritual parts of us. It keeps our bodies physically fit, and..."

"And what, honey?"

Her cheeks burned a raspberry hue. So beautiful. "This may sound silly to you."

He cupped one pretty pink cheek. Her skin was like silk. "Nothing about you is silly to me. Tell me."

She drew in a breath and let it out slowly. "Okay. Our physical bodies house our spiritual selves, Jon. So we must keep our bodies physically fit, because without them we can't move in any direction."

He wanted to kiss her senseless. But he held back, simply let his thumb drift across her luscious lower lip. "Why did you think that would sound silly to me? I'm a personal trainer, Eve. I devote my life to helping people keep their bodies physically fit."

"I don't know," she hedged, "some people think it's kind of a flaky concept. But I believe it, Jonny. Truly I do."

"So do I." He brushed his lips across hers. "You're so beautiful, inside and out. So strong. And I'm adding something to my mission statement as of right now. My new mission statement is to educate, motivate, and support each client by way of an individualized program designed to maximize his physical, emotional, and *spiritual* health."

"Oh..." Her soft sigh drifted over his cheek like the lightest desert breeze.

He lay down on the bed and pulled her against his body. "Tell me what you want, honey." He wanted her to take the lead. He wasn't a submissive. Nothing like that. But he liked a strong woman in the bedroom. He spent all day in control of others' lives. He told them what to eat, how to work out, when to see a medical professional. He didn't mind being in charge. He loved his job. And he certainly wasn't averse to taking the lead in bed. But what really revved his motor was a woman who took what she wanted.

He'd give Eve anything. When he'd returned from turning off his cell phone and she'd demanded he lick her pussy, he'd almost creamed all over himself right there. Eve was the strongest woman he knew. She knew how to get what she wanted in life. Now he wanted her to take what she wanted in the bedroom. From him.

"What do you want, Eve?" His deep voice trembled, and he steadied it. "Tell me."

"Anything you want, Jon." She winked at him.

His cock hardened even further. Damn, she was beautiful. "I want you to take what you're after, gorgeous." He steadied his voice again. "Do whatever you want to me."

"Hmm." Her foggy eyes twinkled. "I do have something in mind, handsome. Lie down."

He complied, the rumpled blankets a soft comfort against his tense, needy body. He waited for another command, but instead she backed toward the door. "Where are you going?"

"Don't worry. I'll be right back." She returned momentarily, her hands filled with several of the smaller scarves she used as color accents on her various dance costumes.

What did she have up her sleeve? Hell, he didn't care. Whatever it was, he was game.

"Grasp the headboard, Jonny."

What? He widened his eyes. She sat on the edge of the bed and fingered the silky fabric. Her chestnut hair fell in soft waves over her shoulders. Curls dangled over her milky breasts. His erection surged in time with his rapid pulse.

"You heard me. You've been begging me to take charge all evening." She leaned forward and brushed her satiny lips against his. "This is something I've always fantasized about. Now grasp the headboard."

Smiling, he did as she demanded. The sheer material floated over his hands and wrists as she bound him.

"There you are," she said, "try moving now."

He could move his wrists but they were tied to the bars of the headboard with some type of hitch. Did she actually know what she was doing?

"Comfortable? Not too tight?"

"No. Not tight at all. But I can't move."

She let out a girlish giggle. "That's the idea."

The husky depth of her voice trickled over him like a smoky cognac warmed in a snifter. She was one hell of a woman.

"Now that you've got me here, honey, what exactly are you going to do with me?"

"Hmm. Well, I know one thing's for certain."

He shivered. "What's that?"

"Eventually, I'm going to fuck the daylights out of you."

His cock was rock-hard. Hard enough to slice through a diamond, no doubt. Jon's arms tensed against the restraints. Damn, he wanted to grab her, kiss her, stuff his cock deep into her hot flesh. But now he was playing by her rules. And God, that turned him on. He burned hotter than blue flame.

She started with moist little kisses to his cheeks and neck. Each touch of her lips scorched him, sent sparks flying to the tip of his sensitive cock. He thrust his hips upward, searching for heat, wet, suction. A welcoming sheath. Such a tease! Eve's soft hair tickled his shoulders and chest like delicate feathers. She trailed her mouth to his and kissed him. A firm kiss, yet a controlled kiss.

"Mmm," she said against his lips. "I shouldn't kiss you. I should tease you. Make you crazy. But I can't resist your beautiful lips, Jonny."

Beautiful? They were too red for a guy. Weird though, women seemed to love them. If Eve loved them, that was okay by him.

"Kissing me is teasing me, honey. Especially when I really want that sweet mouth on my cock."

"Been there, done that." She nipped at his chin and kissed downward to his chest. "You are a magnificent man, Jon. Gorgeous and sculpted." She bit a nipple.

He nearly exploded. "God, Eve."

"I'm going to kiss every inch of you. Every single inch of that muscular physique. Then I'm going to sink my pussy onto your cock. Sound good?" She chuckled against his pecs. She traced a lazy circle around the other nipple.

Was it possible to come without direct stimulation of his penis? Fuck, he was about to find out. Deadly ruby lips tormented him. He would surely die an untimely death here and now. His body flexed, his toes curled. "Eve, damn it, I'm dying here!"

"But what a way to go." Her lips continued their systematic

torture. Over his abs, his hips. "You're in such great shape. How flexible are you, Jonny?"

Flexible? What? "Who cares? Just fuck me, honey."

A soft giggle purred against his hip bone. "I care. Because there's something I want to taste." She spread his legs, moved between them, and gently pushed his thighs forward until they rested against his chest. She smiled. "Nice and flexible, just as I suspected for someone as physically fit as you."

"Eve?"

"Shh." She swirled her tongue over his balls.

They tensed, ready to eject seed into his cock and catapult him over the edge. But her silky tongue slithered downward, teasing that sensitive place under his sac. His whole body quivered. "Honey, please. My God, you have to fuck me. Now!"

Her warm breath massaged his crack. She squeezed first one butt cheek, and then the other. "You have one nice ass, Jonny Blake."

One slender finger taunted his aroused flesh. God no. He'd come if— "Ah!"

She fingered the tight rim.

Mind over matter, damn it. He tensed, held his breath, forced back his climax. Need her. Needed to grab her, pull her forward, force her pretty pink pussy onto his granite cock. Had he truly wanted her to take charge? Damn these restraints!

"Please, Eve. Enough. I want..." He closed his eyes, exhaled the breath he'd been holding.

Magic, magic fingers. She'd called his fingers magic. Fuck, he had nothing on her. She continued her torturous massage, pressing her thumb against his anus, fondling his bottom with the other. He pulled. How strong was this sheer, veily stuff, anyway? No dice. He was at her fucking mercy, and she knew it.

Her mouth covered his balls again as she stroked him with her amazing hands. He groaned, unable to move. She had his arms. She had his legs. He couldn't thrust upward, couldn't...

"Have I brought six-foot-four-inch Jon Blake to his knees?"

"Release me," he growled. "Release me, and I'll fuck you all night long."

Her gorgeous face beamed between his legs. "Not quite yet. I kind of like you like this. Condom?"

"Top drawer."

She left the bed and rummaged in his dresser. She sheathed him, and her fingers fluttered over his cock. He groaned and squeezed his muscles. He wasn't going to blow now, not when she was so close to fucking him. She climbed atop him and sank her warm pussy onto his rigid cock. Sweet surrender.

"Yeah, honey. Just like that. I'm not going to last long."

She leaned forward, teased his lips with her pretty nipples. "Suck it, Jon. Suck my nipple. Get me hotter, baby. Get me burning for you."

Get her hotter? Oh, he'd try. Perfect, perfect tits. He'd lusted after them long before he fell in love with her. Now, with his emotions tied up in his physical longing, her nipples were even more luscious. One tight bud, sweet and hard, pebbled under his tongue. He kissed, nibbled, licked, relishing her moans of approval. God, he wanted his fingers free. Wanted to pluck that other hard nub.

Her hot pussy absorbed his cock. He thrust upward as she rode him, bit her nipple when she moaned. What he wouldn't give to rub her clit for her, make her come.

"Let me go, Eve. Let me make you come."

"Oh, no, baby. I haven't had my fill of this gorgeous, hard cock yet."

Fuck. He had to hold on. Couldn't disappoint her... His hands clenched, he forced his body to calm. Still, she rode him with a wildness he'd never imagined. Her curvy body glimmered with a lacquer of shiny sweat. Her platinum eyes sizzled. He needed to caress her smooth skin, twirl his fingers in her springy chestnut curls.

"Please. I want to touch you."

"You are amazing," she whispered against his forehead before pressing her warm lips to his skin. "I guess you've suffered enough." She sat up and sank down farther onto his hardness.

Ah, sweet friction, though he missed her gorgeous boobs in his face. She sank her fingers into her pubic curls and rubbed her clit. Her beautiful face contorted into a heavenly grimace.

"Yes," she said, her voice a soft sigh. "Right there."

Yeah, honey. Come all over me." He tensed his abdomen and thrust upward into her. "Come. For me."

When her first contraction hugged his cock, he let go. His climax seized him with blinding force, starting with tiny spasms in his balls and then blazing outward along the length of him. He emptied into her, gave her his heart and soul along with his seed. If only...

She came along with him, both of them thrusting, and her sheer beauty mesmerized him. Her tight body tensed, and drips of perspiration fell from her hairline down her cheeks, her neck, her breasts. Her red nipples taunted him, begged for his mouth. When his spasms slowed, he reached for her.

Damn the restraints! "Let me go now, Eve. Please. Let me

hold you."

"Wow, Jonny. That was...wow." She eased off his still-hard cock, slid up his moist body and untied him.

Once free, he wrapped his arms around her and held her against him. He brushed his hands over her sleek, moist shoulders, fondled her swollen breasts, tweaked her puckered red nipples, caressed her thighs, her wet folds. He couldn't touch her enough. Being restrained had made him want her even more.

"I love you so much, Eve."

She didn't respond. He didn't expect it. But he hoped he'd shown her tonight what she meant to him.

"You feel good," she said.

"You do too." He kissed the top of her head, inhaled her exotic bouquet of arousal and sex. The pure love in his heart for this woman overwhelmed him. "And the night is still young."

CHAPTER SIX

Eve spent two days away from the loft. She'd rented a hotel room next to her studio and danced as much as she could.

When she wasn't dancing, she thought about her nights with Jon and Brian. She went over every little detail in her mind. Every kiss, every caress. Every word exchanged. How Brian had introduced her to anal sex, releasing her inhibitions enough that she could try her fantasy of bondage with Jon. Both had given her so much. She had loved being controlled by Brian, had loved controlling Jon. Yet surely something would surface. One little thing that would convince her she loved one more than the other.

Nothing had materialized. She loved them both. Wanted them both. Needed them both.

Flawed. She was definitely flawed.

Now she stood outside the door of the loft she shared with her two best friends. Her two lovers. The two people who meant the world to her. Though she hadn't yet decided between them, she was prepared to make them an offer. An offer she hoped they wouldn't refuse.

She breathed in deeply, let it out slowly, and opened the door. Jon sat on the couch, his head in his hands. Brian sat on the piano bench, his elbows on the ivories. Both so beautiful, both so tortured. All because of her and her stupid-ass flaws. They expected her to choose one or neither of them.

Boy, were they in for a surprise.

"Hi, guys." Her voice trembled.

Jon rose, kissed her on the cheek. Then Brian, his signature kiss to her fingertips. How could she do this?

"I've missed you, sweetheart," Brian said.

"Me too," Jon echoed.

"I've missed you both." No lie. They were all she'd thought about. She paced out of the front room and then back in. "We need to talk."

"We know," Jon said. "We've been waiting."

Tears misted her eyes. "You want to sit down? At the table in the kitchen? Or here?" God, she was rambling. Who cared where they sat?

"How about here?" Jon sat on the front room couch and patted the space next to him. "Sit here, between Bri and me."

"Good idea." Brian plunked onto the other end of the sofa.

Eve sighed and sat down in the middle. She stared straight ahead at the blank screen of the television. "I don't know how to say this."

Brian took her hand and squeezed it. "It's okay, sweetheart. Whatever you decide is fine with Jon and me. We've talked it out, haven't we, bud?"

"Yeah," Jon said. "We know this has been hell for you. It's hell for us too. But we need to know, honey. We need to know if you love either one of us."

She gulped. "That's the problem. I've never fallen in love before."

"Oh." Sadness laced Jon's voice.

"No, let me finish." Eve cleared her throat. "What I mean is, I've had my share of boyfriends, but I never fell in love with any of them. Never felt that solid connection, you know? But now..." She wiped her eyes.

"Damn, don't cry," Jon said.

She sniffed. "It's okay. You need to understand. It happened gradually. I've always loved you guys. You're everything to me. And one day a couple months ago, I realized I'd been thinking about you both all the time. Fantasizing about you. Wanting to be with you intimately."

"Which one of us?" Brian asked.

She let out a harsh sigh. "Don't you get it? Both of you. I'm completely in love with both of you."

Brian dropped her hand. "What exactly are you saying, Eve?"

A vise gripped her heart, and two tears trickled down her cheeks. "I love you both. I spent the last two days ruminating about this, hoping I could find I loved one of you more. Then at least only one of you would be hurting. But I can't. What does that make me? Some fickle little floozy, I guess." She buried her face in her hands and let out the sob she'd been holding back for two days.

Two hips nudged hers. Four arms embraced her. She'd admitted her shortcoming and still they comforted her. "I don't deserve this."

"You're not flawed." Jon's deep voice soothed her. "You're not fickle. You said yourself you've never been in love before. So how can you be fickle?"

"Because it's not normal to be in love with two men. It's not fair to either of you. But I do love you both. You, Brian, your artistic nature, your love of music, the way you make the piano sound as if it's playing just for me."

"It is playing just for you, Eve. When I'm playing it, that is."

"And you're so strong. You know what you want and

you go for it. You have a solid, commanding presence and it's irresistible.

"And you"—she turned to Jon—"so smart and so strong, physically and emotionally. So dedicated to your work, to your friends. You understand your spiritual side. And you're so trusting. You're not afraid to submit to someone else's desires, someone else's needs."

"Only your needs, Eve."

She sighed and closed your eyes. "Both so different, yet so similar in your strength and capacity to love. You're the best of friends. And you're my best friends."

"What are you getting at?" Brian asked.

Always the one to take charge. Brian had to know what was going on. She didn't blame him. "I honestly thought it was only me, that neither of you would ever reciprocate my feelings. I thought I could live with that. Love you both from afar, you know? But then you both tell me you're in love with me and you want me to choose." She gulped. "Well, here it is in black and white. I can't choose one of you over the other."

"No." Jon thumbed her palm. "You're not leaving us, are you? We can go back to the way it was. It's possible, if we all try."

"I...I don't want to go back. It'll hurt too much. And it's not fair to you. You're both amazing."

"Then what?" Brian said. "How are we supposed to deal with this?"

"I—" Her heart pounded like a sledgehammer. What would they think of her? "I have a proposition."

Both bodies tightened next to her. So aware, she was, of each of their movements, each of their emotions. Right now they worried about what she was about to suggest.

"We're listening," Jon said.

"I'll make a decision." She swallowed. The invisible tension pervaded the room and crawled over her skin like tiny fireflies. "But before I do, I'd like to..." *For God's sake, Eve, get a backbone already! You're stronger than this. These men love you as much as you love them. They've proven that.* "I want us to make love." She shivered. She knew she was turning a hundred different shades of red. "Together. All three of us."

Neither of them spoke.

"You think I'm a freak, don't you?"

"Aw, sweetheart," Brian soothed, "you're not a freak. You think Jon or I could love a freak?"

"I just wish..."

"Come on now." He pressed a moist kiss to her neck. "It'll be all right."

"Yeah." Jon nipped at her earlobe. "We'll figure it out."

"Then you're willing...?" Eve's words caught.

Brian's tongue drew circles on her bare shoulder. Jon's firm lips trailed kisses along her jawline. Her sexual hunger stirred to life. Anticipation thickened in the air. They were going to do it. They were going to make love to her together. She sank back against the soft sofa.

"This means the world to me. I can't tell you how much."

Brian eased her camisole over her chest, while Jon fumbled with the snap and zipper of her jeans.

"Oh my God."

"I love you, Eve." Brian lifted her camisole and released her breasts from her bra.

"I love you too, honey." Jon eased her jeans over her hips.

"Okay, bud?" Brian asked.

Jon nodded, removed Eve's sandals, and slid her jeans and

panties off her. The dam broke. Eve wrapped her arms around Brian's neck and kissed him hard.

Jon spread her legs and pressed an open-mouthed kiss to her pussy. "Wet, honey. God, you taste good."

Her tongue tangled with Brian's. She loved how he kissed. So forceful and demanding.

She knew what she wanted. Both of them. And she would take it, if only this once.

She broke the kiss and inhaled a necessary breath. "Your fingers, Jonny. Give me your fingers."

First one thick finger, and then two, breached her wet channel.

"You," she said to Brian.

"Shh. I'm going to suck those sweet nipples, baby. Suck them till they're raw." He bit down hard on one nipple, plucked at the other one.

Fresh cream drizzled onto her thigh.

"Mmm," Jon said. "Whatever you're doing, Bri, keep it up. She's dripping."

"You're delicious," Brian said against her flesh. "I love you, sweetheart."

"Oh, I love you too. Both of you."

The words hung in the air, swirled around her head like a rainbow. How freeing to say them! To speak her heart to the men she loved.

Jon's tousled waves tickled her outer pussy lips, her thighs. Brian's auburn tresses teased the sensitive flesh of her breasts. Shivers racked her body.

"Make her come, Jon," Brian said.

Jon slid a third finger into her cunt and sucked her clit between his gorgeous lips. Her pussy burned from the sweet invasion. Brian's mouth took her whole areola, and she shattered. The climax rocked her, sent tingles from her pussy to her nipples, to every cell in her body. She flew to the stars. Well loved by two men. A miracle, at least for today.

When the spasms subsided, she pulled Jon forward. "Bri," she whispered, "kiss my pussy. Kiss it like you kiss my mouth."

"You want me to lick you, huh, baby? You want my lips on your pretty pussy?"

"God, yes."

"Then beg me. Beg me to kiss your wet cunt."

Brian wanted control. Eve was all too happy to surrender it. "Please, Bri. Please suck my pussy. Make me come."

"My pleasure." He smiled as he and Jon traded places.

"Kiss me, Jonny. I want to taste myself on you."

Jon clamped his mouth to hers and she sucked hard on his tongue. Satiny, delicious. She kissed him deeply, savored her own female musk.

Brian licked her pussy lips, spread them, and thrust his tongue into her. She jolted, kissed Jon harder. Her belly rippled, her skin chilled and then heated. So fucking good. Damn, she was ready to come again. When Brian nipped at her clit, the climax hit her.

She bit down on Jon's tongue, and he groaned into her mouth. So much pleasure. So much love. If only...

Her orgasm continued, forcing her ever higher. She released Jon's mouth and cried both their names. Told them she loved them. Would always love them. Brian tongued her as she eased down.

"We're going to bed now, sweetheart." His voice hummed against her wet thighs. "Both of us. To your bed."

She nodded limply. Both of them in her bed. A dream

come true.

Every cell in her body screamed with sensation. Fresh urgency plowed through her, and liquid heat sizzled beneath her skin. She knew exactly what she wanted. They needed condoms. Two of them. Hell, more than two. And a bed. Hers. Brian was right. It would have to be her bed.

She stood, but her knees buckled beneath her. Jon caught her and gathered her into his arms. He followed Brian to her room. Jon laid her on the bed, the cool sheets a soothing salve to her hot skin.

"How fast can the two of you get naked?"

Pretty fast, apparently. Clothes flew through the room until she had two gorgeous men, four hands, twenty fingers, two rock-hard cocks at her beck and call.

"Oh my..." Her voice had deepened, sounded foreign. Fresh juice rushed between her legs. She reached into her nightstand drawer, pulled out two condoms, ripped them open, and knelt before her two lovers. She tongued Brian's cock, and then Jon's, just enough to coat them with moisture. Then she took one in each hand and slid her fingers back and forth along their solid lengths.

"You're both so beautiful. So handsome. I love you so much."

"I love you, gorgeous," Jon said.

"So do I, sweetheart," Brian said.

Passion surged through her. This was what she had wanted, what she'd asked them for. But apprehension laced the fierce emotion. She was being selfish. This wasn't fair. She backed away.

"Honey?"

She met Jon's dark gaze. His eyes smoldered. He wanted

her. Brian fingered a strand of her hair. His eyes burned. He wanted her too.

She shook her head. "I don't deserve you. Either one of you."

Brian smiled. "Why don't you let us be the judge of that?"

"I agree," Jon said. "Tell us what you want, baby. Maybe we'll give it to you."

Eve closed her eyes. She rolled a condom onto Brian and then onto Jon. "Are you sure?"

They both nodded.

"I want you in my pussy, Jonny," she said.

"Perfect," Brian said. "I'll take your tight ass, sweetheart."

Her body quivered. He'd read her mind.

"Lie down on the bed, Jon." Brian smiled into Eve's eyes, but his commanding tone meant business.

Eve shuddered.

"I want to watch you ride his cock before I take you from behind."

Eve's whole body throbbed. Deep inside her, a hunger burned that she desperately longed to sate. They would satisfy her, these two wonderful men. Perhaps just this once. She hated the self-absorption of it, longed to be able to give as much as she took from them. Yet she didn't have it in her to deny herself supreme satisfaction in the arms of the two men she adored.

Shivering, she climbed onto Jon and sank down on his pulsing cock. "Ah." She closed her eyes as the sigh escaped her throat.

Jon cupped her full breasts. "I love these, Eve. So pretty. The best in the world."

He tugged at her nipples and they hardened into sleek

berries. She rose and sank down again, let his hardness fill her heart.

"That's it, baby," Brian said, his voice deep and husky, "ride his cock. Fuck her good, Jon. Get her all hot, and then I'm going to slide my hard cock up her ass."

Jon thrust his hips upward and his wiry dark hair grazed her clit. Eve shuddered. Sparks ignited across her skin.

"Show him your flutter, sweetheart." Brian was behind her now, his hard chest brushing her back. "Dance for Jonny."

Eve obeyed. She constricted her diaphragm and fluttered, in rhythm with her heartbeat.

"That's beautiful, honey." Jon let out a sigh. "I can feel your muscles, Eve, when you flutter like that, I can feel it on my cock."

"Isn't that awesome?" Brian said, as he worked one finger and then another into her anus. "Man, you're tight. I can't wait to slide into your heat. But first..." He withdrew from her tightness.

Eve let out a sigh of loss. "Bri?"

"Turn her over, Jonny. I want to watch you fuck her hard."

Jon twisted beneath her. "Damn, Bri, when you said that, I almost came."

"No. No coming yet. Not until I say, you understand?"

Jon nodded.

Fingers of pleasure slid over Eve. They were perfect together. One in command, one willing to obey. And it all made her so hot she was ready to detonate. Her entire body throbbed, forcing all the ecstasy straight to her pussy. Strong hands forced her to her back.

Jon, all beautiful strength and muscle, hovered over her, waiting.

"Now," Brian said. "Take her now."

Jon thrust his massive cock into her wet channel. She felt complete, possessed, in the most wonderful of ways.

"That's it, fuck her good, Jonny. Fuck her hard. Harder. Faster."

Jon complied, and with each thrust, Eve edged closer to climax.

"Don't come, sweetheart." Brian's tone reeked of authority. "You either, bud."

"Damn, Bri. I've got to come. She's so tight, so wet."

"No. I'll decide when you come."

"Fuck." Jon continued to pump.

Perspiration dripped from his forehead onto her face. His musk, his vanilla essence, seeped into her.

"Bri," she begged. "Please. I've got to come."

He smiled at her, his beautiful eyes gleaming, and before she had a chance to realize what he was doing, his palm came down with a smack on Jon's taut ass.

"Damn, Bri!" Jon cried out.

Brian reached between their writhing bodies and fingered her clit. "You can come now, Eve." He rubbed her furiously.

Sparks flew over her flesh.

"But you, Jon, not yet."

"Fuck," Jon said. "I can't hold on."

"Oh you can," Brian said. "And you will." He pinched Eve's clit. "Now, baby. Come now."

Eve screamed as she convulsed around Jon's thick cock. So good. So amazing. "God damn. I love you. I love you both!"

"We love you too, sweetheart." Brian patted her clit as she came down.

"I'm dying here," Jon said.

"You're no worse off than I am, pal." Brian stroked Eve's belly, twirling her wetness over her skin in soothing circles.

She panted, trying to catch her breath. The orgasm had literally rocked her world.

"Get on your back, Jon," Brian said. "And you, sweetheart, on top of him. Show him your flutter again."

"If she flutters, I'm going to shoot."

"No you're not."

"Fuck, Brian. I can't hold on any longer."

"You will hold on!" Brian's voice, though still commanding, had softened. But only a bit.

Eve's body still hummed from her release. She could only imagine how Jon was suffering.

"Come on, baby. Get on top of him."

She slid her cunt down on Jon's unyielding shaft. Ah, exquisite stretch.

"How's that feel, Jonny? Isn't she tight after she comes?"

"God. I'm going to burst, damn you." Jon squeezed his eyes shut.

"No, you're not. Ride him, Eve. Flutter."

She nodded and contracted her abdominals in short rapid bursts.

"Shit," Jon said through clenched teeth, his body rigid beneath her.

Brian's lips bussed her neck. "You ready for me, baby?"

Her flutter still going strong, she nodded. Cool lubricant coated her crease. Chills gripped her, followed by the soothing heat of Brian's fingers massaging her tight rim. She breathed in and fluttered again, each rhythmic contraction hitting her clit with a surge of warmth.

"Now, Bri." Her ass was achingly empty. "Take me now."

She ground down onto Jon as Brian nudged her entrance. She sighed when he breached her. "All the way in, Bri."

He kissed her neck. "Say please."

"Please."

Slowly he glided into her. Full. So full. Her body, so full of cock. Her heart so full of love.

"I'm going to fuck you hard, sweetheart. I'm going to pound your pretty ass while Jonny fucks your pussy. Fuck her, Jon. Fuck her good and hard."

Jon thrust upward and Brian pounded from behind.

"Damn, I can feel you fucking her, Bri."

"Me too." Brian's breath puffed against Eve's neck. "God. I never imagined."

Ripples blazed across Eve's skin.

"Pinch her nipples, Jon." Jon pinched one nipple and then the other. His curls teased her clit.

She edged toward the precipice. "I love you. You, Jonny, and you, Bri. Both of you. I love you so much!"

A duet of breathless "I love yous" met her ears. They did love her. She'd never doubt it. To do this for her...

"I'm close," she said, her voice a series of rapid pants.

"Hold on, baby." Brian's whisper slid across her moist neck. "We're all going to come. Together."

"Thank God," Jon rasped. "I'm ready when you are."

Eve ground down onto Jon's cock, rubbed her clit in his bristly curls.

"Now." Brian's stern voice was husky.

The climax zoomed into her. "I love you! God, I love you both!" She let out a ragged groan of release, and a tidal wave of joy carried her into a sea of raw, primal euphoria.

One of Brian's hands locked onto hers. She clutched it to

her breast and laid it on top of Jon's fingers. Brian thrust into her from behind, and his cock convulsed against the tight wall of her ass. Jon plunged upward into her cunt with a violent jerk. Their releases hugged her in thunderous shock waves that rippled through her, adding to her own orgasm.

She rocked with them, swayed with them, danced with them. And when the shudders ceased, they panted together, still joined in body. Still holding hands.

Time stood still. Eve didn't know how many minutes had passed when Brian eased his cock from her ass, pulled her down onto the bed, and nestled her between him and Jon. Two hard, beautiful bodies embraced her. Warmth, satisfaction, sheer passion and emotion. The two men she loved, who each loved her. If only it could last.

But this wasn't reality.

"That was wonderful," she said. "Thank you both. Thank you so much."

Jon brushed his lips against her cheek, tickling her with his stubble. "Thank you, honey. That was amazing."

"Yeah," Brian agreed, taking her hand. "It sure was."

"You both mean everything to me," she said.

"You mean everything to us too," Jon said.

"The thing is..." Eve drew a deep breath. "I said I'd make a decision after we made love. But...I can't. I can't decide between the two of you. I know it's selfish, but I want you both."

Brian chuckled against her hair. "You're not selfish, Eve. You're just in love."

"But—"

"You have any complaints, Jon?" Brian asked. "About what just happened?"

Eve turned to Jon, whose dark eyes twinkled.

"Not a one."

"Are you both serious? This isn't—"

"Conventional? No," Brian said. "But I have to tell you, that was the best sex I've ever had."

"Me too," Jon agreed, "hands down."

"You mean you want to be...together? All of us?"

Brian kissed her forehead. "It's not originally what either of us had in mind, but we discussed it before you got home. We both agreed if you were up to it, we'd give it a try. We even talked a little about what we like in the bedroom. After all, Jon and I have been best friends forever. We love each other, though not in that way. And we both love you. Want you as a friend and as a lover."

"So when I suggested a threesome...?"

"We were all for it," Jon said.

Eve smiled, caressed Brian's thigh, Jon's taut abs. "And I was scared you'd think I was a freak for wanting to try it."

"If you hadn't suggested it," Brian said, "we would have."

"Oh..." Pleasure gripped her. Love filled her heart. She sat up in bed and looked down at her lovers. "I've got to be the luckiest woman on the planet. What can I do for you? Anything. I'll cook you a gourmet feast. I'll even make it healthy, Jonny. I'll serve you breakfast in bed. I'll suck both your cocks at the same time. Anything. I'll give you anything."

Brian's eyes pierced her with emerald fire. Jon's burned her with dark embers. They spoke in unison.

"Dance for us."

Slow and Wet

SLOW AND WET

"Slow and wet, darlin', slow and wet. You know just what I like."

Jillian grinned against the steel of Dale's gorgeous cock. Oh, yeah, she knew what her man liked. And she liked it too. That was her naughty secret to giving the fantastic head Dale adored. Concentrate on what felt good to her tongue and lips, and his pleasure would follow. Right now, licking every inch of his erection felt sweet as honey-lemonade on a hot summer day.

Jill swirled her tongue along his length, up over his cock head, and tormented him with long, wet strokes. When she reached the base, she circled around his sac, savoring every moan, every sigh from his firm, full lips as she cupped him and sucked each ball into her mouth.

"You're killin' me," Dale said, his voice low and husky.

Jill smiled again, twirled her tongue around his sac, and licked up the long shaft to tease him underneath. She flicked her tongue over his cock head and sucked it between her lips.

He moaned. "Damn, Jill. You give great head."

Flexing her tongue into a point, she fucked his tiny slit. Once. Twice. Three times. He grabbed her cheeks, fisted his hands into her auburn tresses, and pulled her forward, forcing her to take his entire length. She devoured him, his salty manliness an enticing flavor. But only for a few seconds. Jill liked to be in control when she sucked Dale, so she eased back and twirled her tongue over the sensitive head of his penis. She resisted the urge to take him in her hands, to curl her fingers around his steely hardness.

Instead, she rained tiny kisses along his length. With each of his trembles, her pulse quickened. Nothing turned her on more than turning him on. Taking his cock head into her mouth again, she let it rest against her bottom lip while she flicked her tongue over the top. Slowly, she crept forward, her lips molding around his hot cock. She increased her suction just a little, and then stopped and backed off every now and again, teasing him. When he grabbed her head again, the muscles in his forearms taut with tension, she took pity on him and took another rigid inch into her mouth.

"Just a little farther, darlin'. God, that's good, the way you suck me."

Each time he tried to pull her forward, she retaliated by taking an inch away. Smiling against his hardness, a tiny giggle escaped her throat. The vibration must have tickled him because he shuddered and growled out a low curse. She gave in and took another inch. His cock felt hot and moist in her mouth, and she loved it. Loved him, though she hadn't told him.

Dale Cross was her cowboy. Her lover. Her Prince Charming. Her destiny. He just didn't know it yet.

Her hips undulated in rhythm with her soft thrusts on his cock, and with each forward motion, she imagined him sinking that rock-hard length into her moist pussy. She was already wet. Had been since he'd greeted her with a kiss when she showed up at his place to surprise him. She'd been out of town on business for a week and hadn't been able to wait a minute longer to see her man.

And now she couldn't wait a minute longer to fuck him. She wanted his hardness inside her, stretching her. She took his entire shaft into her mouth one last time, letting the knob of his cock head graze the back of her throat.

He groaned, shivering against her, his dark nest of curls tickling her lips and chin. Her pulse raced with the urge to finish him this way, to let him erupt in her mouth so she could taste his salty cum as it slid down her throat.

But no. She wanted to fuck. Now. Though sorry to let it go, she removed her lips from his hard length. It stood erect in all its glory, shiny from her saliva, its golden color marbled with two veins meandering around its thickness. Dale Cross had the most beautiful cock Jill had ever seen.

She pushed him onto his back and started to climb on top of him for a ride, but suddenly found herself on her own back, her cowboy staring down at her with mischief in his eyes.

"Hey, Dale. I wanted to fuck."

"Darlin'"—is brown eyes gleamed at her—"I promise you the fuck of the century. Later. Right now I want to taste that sweet pussy."

Jill sighed and relented. As much as she loved fucking Dale and sucking his cock, having him lick her pussy was right up there on the feel-good scale too.

Dale smiled between her legs, pulled each thigh over his shoulders, and buried his face in her wetness. He sucked pussy the way he did everything—with a singular purpose and motivation to be the best. From his bronc busting, to babysitting his niece and nephew, to helping his grandmother run the ranch that would be his someday—he tackled each job that came his way with effort and finesse. Goose bumps formed on Jill's body, and her nipples stiffened when his silky tongue slid over her slick pussy lips. He nibbled at her clit, bringing her almost to the precipice, and then backed off, teasing her.

"Please, Dale. Let me come."

"You'll get what's comin' to you, darlin'," he said. "You drove me insane with your cock suckin'." His lopsided grin, lips shiny with her juices, tantalized her from between her thighs.

She met his smoldering gaze. "That's not fair, Dale."

"Not fair?" He chuckled and nipped her thigh. "I'll show you not fair. I'm gonna kiss your hot pussy till you scream, lady. How's that for not fair?" He dove back into her cunt, licking and nibbling.

Jill cupped her breasts, squeezed them, and plucked her hard nipples. The sensation traveled at light speed and landed between her legs, adding to the torment Dale was inflicting on her. He sucked at her, and the smacking of his tongue and lips made her tingle.

"Damn, you sure are wet," he said against her folds. "So wet for me. So juicy. I guess you missed me, huh?"

"Y-Yes. I missed you more than I can say. Now please let me come."

He shook his head, and his wavy dark curls tickled her inner thighs. "I missed you too, Jill. I missed your hot kisses, your tasty nipples, your sweet pussy." He flicked his tongue over her clit and then dragged it downward through her folds, all the way to her anus, where he swirled it in lazy circles.

She shivered.

"Mmm," he said. "When are you gonna give me your ass, darlin'?"

"I... I don't know." She couldn't think about that now. All she could think about was coming. She feared she might explode into a million pieces if he didn't let her release.

His laugh rumbled against her ass cheeks as he fingered her tight hole. "I got it nice and lubed up right now. Let me just..."

Jill gasped as he penetrated her.

"Just a finger. Relax."

She loved this man, and she wanted to please him. She loosened and found she liked the feeling of his thick finger sliding in and out of her ass.

"You're so pretty, darlin'," he said. "So pink and puckered. I'm gonna fuck your pussy today. And someday," he sighed, his voice a heady rumble, "you're gonna let me sink my cock into your virgin ass, and we're both going to love every second of it."

"Sure, Dale, sure." Jill was pretty certain she'd agree to anything right now, if he'd just let her come.

"Promise, darlin'? Promise you'll let me fuck your ass someday?"

"Dale..."

"It doesn't have to be today. But I want you so much. I want to claim every part of you."

"Yes, Dale. Fine. Just. Please. Let. Me. Come."

The hot breath from his laugh tickled her clit. "You've been a good girl. You deserve a reward." His finger still penetrating her ass, he lowered his mouth to her pussy and sucked the whole swollen fruit into his mouth while he tongued her clit.

She exploded, and her womb convulsed. The spasms radiated outward, until every nerve ending in her body sizzled. Still he fingered her ass, and the intense pressure added to her blazing climax. She soared as the ripples surged through her body. "Dale!" she cried. "That feels so good. So fucking good!"

He licked her folds, and she floated downward, her body sinking into the softness of his bed. His finger left her ass and he tongued her once, twice more, before he crawled upward and crushed his mouth to hers in a searing kiss. He tasted of the crisp honey-lemonade they had shared, spiced with her female musk. Intoxicating. Their tongues dueled and tangled, their breaths mingled, until he ripped his lips from hers, panting.

"Condom," he said, and extended his arm and fumbled in his nightstand drawer. A few seconds later, sheathed, he plunged into her hot, willing cunt.

Jill let out a soft sigh as her walls clamped around him. Good. So damn good. Like he was born to fill her. A perfect fit.

"Darlin', you're so tight right after you come. So hot."

His voice, deep and hoarse, swirled around her like a smoky bourbon. So fucking sexy. He pulled out and thrust into her again, his hardness sliding along the swollen nub of her clit. She squeezed her legs together and hugged his hips as he drove his cock harder and harder into her. Each time he pulled out, she whimpered until he drove back in.

"So tight, Jill. So fuckin' tight."

With each thrust, she longed to cry out her true feelings of love for him. Was it too soon? They'd only been seeing each other a couple months. But with each kiss of his lips, each stroke of his long, hard cock, Jill knew, without a doubt, that she was in love with Dale Cross. The way he worshiped her body, made love to her soul, he had to feel the same way.

Didn't he?

She grabbed the firm cheeks of his bottom.

He groaned. "Yeah, Jill. I love when you play with my ass."

She squeezed him and pushed downward, forcing him farther into her heat. "Dale," she panted, as her climax ascended, "Dale, I—"

"Jillian, I can't hold on any longer," he rasped. "I'm sorry, darlin', I wanted you to come again... God!" He thrust into her one last time, releasing.

Her orgasm hit her as his hot cum shot into the condom. She spasmed around him.

"Yeah, yeah," he said. "You're coming too. I'm glad. So glad..." He kissed her neck with firm, moist lips. "Damn, I've missed you."

Jill's whole body quivered from her climax, from his sweet kiss, but mostly from his admission that he'd missed her. She'd missed him so much she'd gotten a speeding ticket getting back home to see him. The job offer she'd received—complete with significant pay increase—to relocate back to Denver paled in comparison to life here with Dale. She'd say no first thing tomorrow.

"Give me a few minutes, darlin'," he said, "and I'll be good to go again. I'll last longer next time, I promise." He slid off her slick body onto his back and reached for her.

She snuggled into his arms and inhaled his intoxicating blend of cinnamon, cedarwood, and male musk. Dale never wore cologne. Jill breathed in the spicy aroma again. Mmm. If he could bottle his own fragrance, he'd make a fortune.

She lifted her head and took in his sculpted chest, the dark hairs curling over his nipples matted with the sheen of his sweat. He looked good enough to eat. Again.

He tilted his head toward her. "You want some more lemonade, darlin'?"

She nodded and stretched her arms over her head. "I've got a thirst to quench, that's for sure, cowboy."

The adorable dimple in his right cheek twinkled at her when he smiled. "Sit tight. I'll be right back with a cool drink."

Jill watched his lean backside as he strode out of the

bedroom. He was so handsome, with a face and body like a god. She could look into his beautiful bronze eyes forever and never tire of their piercing fire.

She stretched again and let her body sink into the cool cotton sheets covering Dale's king-sized bed. A bed she hoped to occupy for a long, long time. Her fingers wandered to her nipples and she stroked them, bringing each to a tight bud. Mmm. So good. She plucked at them lazily, imagining Dale's talented lips sucking each one. She let one hand drop and graze her swollen clit. Her pussy was still soaked, and she rubbed the smooth folds between her fingers. Within minutes, she was close to climax again.

But where was Dale? How long did it take to pour two glasses of honey-lemonade, anyway? "Dale?" She sat up, her pussy still pulsing with the need to come. But why go at it alone? She'd just as soon bring herself to orgasm with Dale's hard cock in her mouth. And this time she'd swallow him whole and feel his hot cum trickle across her tongue.

She stood and ambled out the door. "Cowboy, I'm still horny, and it's going to take more than your famous honey-lemonade to cool me off—"

She stopped abruptly in Dale's kitchen, her words dangling in midair. Dale stood at the counter, his back to her, wearing green cotton boxers. When had he put them on? But her boyfriend's attire was the least of Jill's concerns.

At the table sat another cowboy nearly as hot as Dale himself. And not a thread of clothing covered her.

The blond cowboy's lips curved into a grin as he ran his long fingers through his tousled hair. Lapis lazuli eyes raked over Jill's nude body.

"Seems I've been gone too long, Dale," he said. "The

scenery's definitely changed around here"—he arched a nutmeg eyebrow—"for the better."

Jill's skin heated, and she crossed her arms over her puckering nipples. She couldn't help staring at the broad chest clothed in a black western shirt. The first few snaps were open, and several golden chest hairs peeked out.

Dale turned around and his jaw dropped. "Jill!" He rushed toward her, pulled her into his arms, and shielded her private parts from the other cowboy's view.

"We used to share everything, Dale," the blond said with a husky laugh.

"Go get something on," Dale whispered in her ear.

"I heard that," the man said, still smiling, "and I've already seen her gorgeous tits and her pretty red nipples." He cleared his throat. "And what's down below. Why not introduce us?"

"Be happy to," Dale said, "once she's properly covered."

The other cowboy ignored Dale and stood, offering his hand. His denims hugged hips as lean as Dale's. If he turned around, she'd no doubt see an ass just as fine too. He was almost as tall as Dale, which made him six-two, at least.

"I'm Travis Logan..." His voice was slightly deeper than Dale's, with a little more of a cowboy twang. "Dale's best friend since we were kids, and you're the prettiest thing I've seen in a month of Sundays."

The bold words sashayed around Jill's heated body, and her already hard nipples stiffened further and poked into Dale's golden chest. Dale's cock came to life inside his boxers and brushed against her tummy.

An icy tingle raced through her. Amazing, how Dale could affect her so. Or was it Travis? Couldn't be.

"Trav, don't you have any shame?"

"You've known me almost my whole life, so you know the answer to that question." Travis grinned. His full pink lips were nearly as luscious as Dale's.

"Yeah, I guess I do," Dale said. "Trav, this is my girl, Jillian Reynolds."

A rush of warmth coursed through Jill at the words "my girl".

"Mighty pleased to make your acquaintance, ma'am." Travis squeezed her hand.

A flare of heat skittered over her skin.

"Seems Dale has all the luck. Beautiful women have always flocked to him."

Jill leaned farther into Dale's chest, but Travis continued to hold her hand, rubbing his thumb into her palm. His touch felt nice. Which wasn't good. She whisked her hand away.

"Remember the good old days?" He spoke to Dale, but he stared at Jill, dropping his gaze to her breasts, which were still crushed against cowboy number one. "When we did everything together?"

Dale cleared his throat. "I remember."

"We were team ropers," Travis said to Jill. "Champions. Started when we were kids. Couple years ago, though, I went solo in ropin', and Dale here switched to bustin' broncs. I've been away since then, tourin' the circuit."

"And you, Dale?" Jill raised her gaze to his brown eyes.

"You know where I've been, darlin'. Here, helpin' my grandma run this place. Doin' the local rodeos."

"But didn't you ever want to tour?"

"Heck, no. I'm a homebody. I'm happy here, runnin' the ranch"—he smiled—"hangin' out with you." He turned to Travis. "Jill's from Denver."

"I took you for a big-city gal," Travis said. "What are you doin' in a little cow-town like Sweetwater Junction, Wyoming?"

"I'm in computer sales. A few months ago, an opportunity came up to relocate here, and I jumped at it. I wanted to get away from the hustle and bustle."

Travis chuckled and shook his head. "If only I'd come home sooner, I might have seen you first." He winked. "'Course that didn't always matter."

"Trav..."

Jill's heart raced beneath her chest. Why? From being held in Dale's strong arms, no doubt. Or was something else going on?

Naked. Shit, she was still naked.

"Uh, Dale? I need to—"

"Yeah, you sure do, darlin'." He grabbed her rump and lifted her, and she wrapped her legs around his waist. "We'll be back in a minute, Trav. Fully clothed."

"Damn," Travis said. "Can't say I've seen enough of the beauty of my hometown just yet."

"Yeah, you have," Dale said, walking back to the bedroom. He looked over his shoulder. "You've seen all of Jill you're gonna see, pal."

"Don't be so sure about that, buddy."

Had Jill imagined the words? Or had they actually come from the gorgeous blond cowboy? She tightened her thighs around Dale's sexy waist. Didn't matter anyway. She needed to get dressed and then douse herself with about a gallon of Dale's honey lemonade. Then maybe go jump into Sweetwater Lake.

And she wasn't even sure that would cool her off today.

★ ★ ★ ★

"It wouldn't hurt to ask her, you know."

Dale sprinkled seasoned salt on the three sirloin cuts, flipped them carefully, and poked Jill's to make sure it wasn't too done. His girl liked her steak oozing. He turned to Travis and tried to look nonchalant despite the hairs on the back of his neck standing tall.

"She's a nice girl, Trav. She wouldn't be into that."

"Lorna was a nice girl too. Remember? She was my girl, Dale, but you took many turns with her, and it was fun for all of us."

"That was years ago."

"Four years, buddy. We had some good times. We were a team."

"We were team ropers, Travis. Not team fuckers."

Travis tossed his head back and let out a guffaw. "I seem to recall we did pretty well in the team fuckin' department too. Lorna never had any complaints, and neither did any of the others."

"This is different."

"How so?"

"She's..." Dale hedged. Words he couldn't form stuck in the back of his throat.

"I can tell she's special to you."

"Yeah." He cleared his throat and poked at a steak that really didn't need poking. "Aw hell, I don't know."

Travis took a long sip of his honey-lemonade and shook his head. "I never thought I'd see the day."

"See what day?"

"Nothin'. Never mind." Travis arched one eyebrow. "This

is your chance to give her a hell of a gift, bud. Two huge cocks for the price of one."

"I'm all the cock she needs. Besides, haven't we outgrown all that?"

"Outgrown the desire to give a woman the ultimate pleasure? Heck, I sure haven't. Why not let her make the decision?"

Dale shrugged. He couldn't deny he'd been aroused at the way Travis had raked his gaze over Jill's nude body. His sex had stiffened in his drawers and pushed into Jill's soft flesh. Watching his friend fuck his woman appealed to him on a primal level. But what really turned him on was the thought of offering her something purely physical, purely hedonistic. Purely for her ultimate pleasure, as Travis had said. Would Jill want something like that?

Lorna had wanted them both, and Travis had allowed it. Dale poked the steaks once more and then transferred them to a platter. He looked over his head to see Jill push open the sliding glass door.

"The salad and veggies are ready whenever you two are." Her smile lit up her gorgeous face, and her auburn hair fell in ringlets around her creamy shoulders.

"We're comin' now, darlin'," Dale said, glancing sideways at Travis.

But Travis didn't catch Dale's eye. His gaze was settled on Jill.

★ ★ ★ ★

Both Travis and Dale had stared at her all through dinner. Now, her back turned as she loaded the dishwasher, the heat of their dual gazes still penetrated her like the Wyoming sun on a cloudless summer day.

"Jill?"

She turned at Dale's voice. "Yeah?"

"Trav has a few things to take care of."

"Oh, of course." She cleared her throat and advanced toward the two men, her arm extended to Travis. "It was great to meet you. I'm sure I'll see you again soon."

Travis's husky chuckle eased over her as his large calloused hand enclosed hers. "Soon, yes, I hope. I'll be back later tonight, if all goes well." He pulled her toward him and gave her a chaste kiss on the cheek, shook Dale's hand, and then headed out the front door of the ranch house.

Jill stared into Dale's bronze eyes, puzzled. "What did he mean, 'if all goes well'?"

Dale took her hand. "Come on. Mabel'll be here in the morning to clean the kitchen. You know you don't need to do this."

"But I don't mind—"

"I do," he said, and led her into the living room. He sat down on his rustic leather couch and patted the soft cushion next to him.

She sat, and he gathered her into his arms and kissed her neck.

"You didn't answer my question. Is Travis staying with you tonight?" Jill's muscles tensed, she wasn't sure why, as she waited for his answer. Did she want Travis to stay?

Dale let out a short cough. "No. Not the whole night, anyway. He, uh, has a place not far from here where he hangs his hat when he's in town."

"Oh. Well, maybe we'll see him tomorrow."

"Nope. While we were grillin' the steaks, he told me he was leavin' come sunup for another rodeo gig."

Jill swallowed, a strange sense of loss nagging at her. She quickly batted it away. So she wouldn't see Travis again. Dale was the man she loved. He was inside her, a part of her. She breathed in, catching his masculine scent. She'd do anything for Dale Cross.

"Thing is, darlin'," Dale continued, "Travis was wonderin'..."

"Wondering what?" Why would Travis wonder anything that mattered to her and Dale? A chill slithered across the back of her neck, and her sex responded. Strange.

Dale stood abruptly. "I'll be right back."

"Well...okay." She watched his gorgeous denim-clad ass as he walked back to the kitchen. Magnificent.

He returned a few minutes later with two glasses of lemonade and handed one to her. "I put a shot of bourbon in, the way you like it."

Jill took a sip of the crisp beverage. "Thanks. Now what's going on?"

Dale took a long, slow drink of his lemonade. "There's something I want you to know about me, Jill. Something I want to share with you."

"Okay." Nervous ripples skittered across her skin. The thought that Dale had hidden something from her agitated her. She loved him. Would marry him if he asked. And now? She inhaled, bracing herself.

"Travis and I...well..." He stood again and paced to the end of the room and back.

"Dale, for God's sake, what the hell is going on?"

He gazed into her eyes, his own burning with fire. He

cupped her cheeks in his strong hands and leaned down and pressed his lips to hers in a gentle kiss. Jill's heart leaped into overdrive. She opened to him, let his smooth tongue entwine around hers. What started as gentle soon became passionate and lusty.

Dale ripped his mouth away. "Damn, I can't even kiss you without losing my mind."

Her nerves settled—a bit—and she let out a laugh. "And that's a bad thing?"

"No. No, not at all." He sat back down next to her and took her hand, massaging each finger. "I want to give you everything, darlin'. You're so damn special to me. And there's somethin' I can give you that... Well, I don't know if you want it."

"I'd love anything you gave me, Dale." Especially if it's circular in shape and symbolizes forever.

He smiled, his eyes crinkling. "Travis is attracted to you, darlin', and the two of us, well... We'd like to make love to you, if you're willin'."

Ice prickled Jill's skin, even as her pussy warmed. She was taken aback, but also turned on. Two men? Two hot men? But she was in love with Dale. Why would he want this? And was it wrong for the idea to intrigue her? Make her hot? Because it did indeed make her hot, despite her feelings for Dale, and Dale alone.

"You would share me?"

He lifted her hand and gently slid his lips across her palm.

Her tummy fluttered.

"It's not sharing you, not really. It's giving you a night of pleasure. Pure, unadulterated pleasure. Something I can't give you alone. Two mouths to kiss you. Two cocks to fuck you, darlin'. But if you don't want it, that's okay."

"And you've...you've done this before?"

"Yes."

"And enjoyed it?"

"Yes. I've enjoyed giving a woman that amount of pleasure. And the woman has always been extremely satisfied."

A knife of jealousy stabbed her. She didn't like thinking of Dale with other women. But heck, she was no virgin herself. Of course he'd had other women before her. She nervously swiped at the beads of condensation on her glass of lemonade.

"And you and Travis don't...with each other?"

He smiled, and a chuckle escaped. "No, darlin'. That's not what this is about. We both love givin' a woman the ultimate sexual experience. It's for you, not for us." He let out a shaky laugh. "Well, a little for us, I guess. I'd love seein' you like that, Jill. I'd love to be able to give it to you."

Naked between two beautiful men? The idea had merit. Ménages had starred in her fantasies on more than one occasion. But with Dale? The man she loved? He looked at it as a gift. Something he wanted to give her. And though she wanted to accept—oh yeah, she really wanted to accept— would it change his opinion of her? Would he look at her the same way afterward? Would he ever fall in love with her, feel about her the way she did about him?

Jill gulped the rest of her drink and handed the glass to Dale. "No more. At least not laced."

"Okay, Jill." Dale's tone reeked of resignation. "I understand."

"I'm not sure you do," she said, as she feathered her fingers over his forearms, his sinewy muscle tripping her pulse.

She was wet. She wanted this. An experience she'd never forget. A precious gift from the man she loved.

And if he couldn't love her back? She'd relish this night. And tomorrow she'd pick herself up, dust herself off, and take that job offer.

"I don't want to be drunk tonight, Dale. I want to feel every slide of those four hands, every pucker of those two mouths, every thrust of those two big cocks."

He smiled. "I promise you, darlin', this'll be a night you'll never forget."

★ ★ ★ ★

"Any ground rules?" Travis asked, as four strong and capable hands gently peeled the clothes from Jill's body.

A soft summer breeze cooled the Wyoming summer night, and the moon veiled the threesome in delicate light. Dale's backyard was enclosed, private, and carpeted with soft grass. The men had laid a king-sized cotton throw on the ground. When Dale didn't answer right away, Jill's flesh heated. Ground rules? What were they talking about?

"You can do whatever she wants you to do," Dale said. "But her ass is mine."

"Understood."

As her naked body was exposed, determination overcame her shyness. Heck, Travis had already seen her naked. She wouldn't think. She'd just feel, and she'd top any previous ménage these two cowboys had orchestrated.

She fingered the snaps on Dale's shirt and ripped them open, letting her fingers wander over the dark hair dusting his sculpted chest. She bent and flicked her tongue over one copper nipple, and her pussy jerked as the nub hardened under her lips. She tugged on it, Dale's groans fueling her desire, as she unbuckled his belt and unzipped his jeans. She pushed them down his strong thighs, and he stepped out of them.

Looking over her shoulder, she saw that Travis had also undressed. Light golden hair covered his muscular chest and well-formed legs. His cock, slightly longer than Dale's but not quite as thick, jutted from a bush of dark blond curls. Moisture trickled down her thigh.

She turned back to Dale, and he took her mouth in a searing kiss. As their tongues tangled, hard flesh pressed against her back, and a second pair of lips trailed tiny moist kisses over her shoulder. She shuddered and her skin tingled. Dale's hard cock pressed into the soft flesh of her tummy, while Travis's nudged her back. Dale cupped her breasts and squeezed them, and he eased her down to her knees. His mouth still clamped to hers, he pressed his cock against her, as Travis did the same from behind.

When Dale finally broke the kiss, panting, Travis nudged her shoulder, pressed her onto her back, and leaned over her and took her mouth. His kiss tasted of passion and fire, while Dale's had tasted of intensity and emotion. His tongue had a rougher texture than Dale's, and Jill found she enjoyed the different sensation. He used less tongue than Dale, but his kiss was no less intoxicating.

Dale trailed his lips along her neck, up to her earlobe, where he nipped her. She shuddered. But just as she deepened her assault on Travis's mouth, her lips locking his, Dale yanked her away by the shoulder. The suction of the kiss broke with a loud smack.

"New ground rule," Dale said huskily. "You don't kiss her."

Jill didn't hear Travis's response, if there was one, because Dale crushed his mouth to hers in a kiss so passionate and possessive it erased all memory of Travis's lips. Dale's tongue tasted of honey, of spice, of sweet love, and Jill drowned in the pleasure of his kisses.

When he finally ripped his mouth from hers, Travis sat over her with a pitcher of honey-lemonade.

"Dale told me this is your favorite drink, sweetheart," he said, a glint in his bright blue eyes. "We thought you might enjoy a little tonight."

"I'd love some." Jill smiled and looked around. "Looks like you forgot the glasses, though."

"Who needs glasses?" Dale said, his tone teasing. "Go ahead, Trav."

Travis tipped the pitcher, and the liquid trickled onto Jill's hot body. She squealed, and her nipples puckered into tight buds. The cool beverage flowed over her breasts, her belly, her thighs, easing between her legs and into her wet folds.

"Now I guess we'll have to clean you up, darlin'," Dale drawled.

"It'll be a pleasure," Travis said. He cupped the breast on his side and thumbed a hard nipple. "She sure has pretty tits. The nicest I've seen in some time."

"Mmm-hmm." Dale bent to taste one. "Sweet and red and hard as pearls." He licked the tip of her nipple.

Jill moaned, shuddering.

"Two mouths, darlin'." Dale's breath vibrated against her flesh. "Two pairs of lips to kiss you. Two tongues to lick all that syrupy lemonade off your hot body."

Travis's firm lips latched onto the other tight bud. His touch was lighter than Dale's. He licked where Dale sucked. And Jill found she loved each sensation. Warmth spread through her breasts and flashed to her pussy, which pulsed between her thighs.

Dale tugged, and Travis kissed, and Jill thought she'd implode with want. After lingering moments of vivid stimulation that trickled to her sex, she needed more. The nipple Travis licked wanted to be bitten, and the one Dale nipped wanted to be licked.

"Could you guys switch places? Each suck the other nipple?"

"Anything you want," Dale said, his voice hoarse. "This is for you."

They quickly switched, and Jill sighed and sank farther into the moist cotton, her nipples tight with anticipation. The smacks and slurps of the two luscious masculine mouths sent shivers across her skin.

"Mmm, gorgeous." Travis's deep voice rumbled against her sensitive flesh. "The tart lemon mixed with your sweet flesh."

"Yeah, delicious. And beautiful," Dale agreed, and tugged harder with his teeth.

The pleasure shot to her cunt with lightning intensity. "Such pretty red nipples, so tangy from the lemonade," Travis said, "and I bet that's not all that's pretty and red."

"And tangy," Dale added.

Cream oozed from her pussy. She was wet and swollen and ripe for the plucking.

Dale released her nipple with a soft pop, leaned forward, and thrust his tongue into her mouth for a scorching kiss. The fresh citrus taste of the lemonade he'd sucked exploded in a candied bouquet. He trailed moist kisses over her cheek, down the hill of her breast to her tummy. He swirled his tongue into her navel while Travis continued to lick her other nipple.

Her body heated, chilled, and heated again. She writhed under the expert hands and mouths.

When Dale reached her patch of russet curls, he spread her legs and groaned. "You're swollen and red. So pretty. Will you show Travis your pussy, darlin'? Let him lick you?" Dale's eyes smoked a deep umber.

Jill's body ached for a cock. Any cock. Travis's cock. "I want Travis to lick me. To take me."

Travis released Jill's nipple and smiled against her fleshy breast. "It'll be my pleasure." He moved to join Dale.

Her legs spread wide, Jill watched the two heads—one dark, one blond—eye her pussy with rapt attention.

"She's delicious, Trav." Dale swiped his tongue over her clit.

A zing of heat slid up her spine.

"Taste her."

Travis bent down and slithered his rough tongue over her clit. Again, she noted the different textures of their two tongues. Both drove her crazy with lust. Dale slid his fingers up and down her slick labia, squeezing them together, while Travis continued to nip at her clit.

"Gorgeous, darlin'," Dale said. "Just gorgeous. You've got the prettiest pussy I've ever seen. How does it feel, Jill? How does it feel to have me play with your lips while Trav licks your clit?"

Feel? How could she put it into words? Amazing wouldn't begin to describe it. "Mmm," she said. "Dale, I can hardly breathe it feels so fantastic."

His chuckle rumbled against her thigh, sticky from the lemonade and her own cream. He nipped her there and continued to slide his fingers over her slick folds. She writhed, searching for her release, but Travis's lips denied it. Every time she was about to come, he released her clit and kissed her belly.

"Dale," she panted. "I want... I need..."

Two of Dale's thick fingers thrust inside her pussy, and she shattered, clenching around him in sweet convulsions.

"Come for me, darlin'," he said. "Just like that. Milk it. Cream all over my fingers."

Once her spasms slowed, Dale removed his fingers and shoved his hot tongue into her willing flesh. "I'm suckin' the honey out of you, darlin'," he said against her wet pussy. "Every last drop."

Travis moved forward, took a hard nipple into his mouth, and licked gently. "You've got one sweet pussy, Jill," he said against her breast. "Dale's a lucky man."

"Mmm. I sure know it." Dale swiped his tongue through her labia once more and then nipped her clit, sending an aftershock shuddering through her. "Get a condom, Trav," he said. "I want you to take her first. She's so fuckin' tight right after she comes. You're gonna love it." He looked up at Jill, his eyes burning into her. "That okay with you, darlin'?"

God, yes. "Please. Take me, Travis."

Travis released Jill's nipple. "Don't have to twist my arm." A minute later, Travis knelt between her legs, sheathed and ready to plunge into her. "You sure, bud?" He nodded at Dale, who was kneeling behind Jill's head, his cock dangling in front of her lips.

"I'm sure," Dale said, "if it's what Jill wants."

Jill panted, and her eyes blurred. She wanted that cock, wanted those dark blond curls to tickle her labia as he drove into her. "Yes." Jill puffed against Dale's engorged shaft. "Fill me up. Now."

"You got it, sweetheart." Travis entered her in one smooth thrust.

"Ah, yes." Jill's walls clenched onto Travis's hardness. Different than Dale. But big, and hard, and hot. The feelings were different too. More primal, more urgent, completely focused on pleasure for pleasure's sake.

"Let him fuck you, darlin'," Dale said. "Concentrate on the physical. I want you to feel good."

"Mmm, I do, Dale." She reveled in the raw joy of being taken.

Travis's skillful pounding held her body in thrall. But Dale's words, his deep timbre, his concern for her enjoyment, bewitched her and filled her heart with unimaginable sensation.

"Would you suck me while he fucks you?" Dale's cock nudged her lips. "Would you let me fuck your sweet mouth while Travis fucks your pussy?"

"Cowboy, you know I'll always suck you," Jill said, and she twirled her tongue over his head. She licked off the bead of pre-cum and savored the saltiness. "Mmm. I love how you taste."

"I bet I'm not near as tasty as you are," he said. "Yeah, that's it. Suck me. Suck my cock."

Jill craned her neck to take more of his manhood between her lips. He knelt above her, and she licked the underside of his swollen length. She inhaled the muskiness of his balls and lapped at them, tonguing every peak and valley of his sac.

"You drive me crazy," Dale said, panting.

She lowered her head back to the soft blanket and licked his cock head some more. "I love your cock, Dale. I love to suck it."

All the while Travis pumped into her, and her pussy

creamed over him as she neared the precipice again.

"You're getting close, sweetheart," Travis said. "You're pussy's clenching. Damn, you feel good. Such a sweet fuck."

"Do you want to come all over Trav's big cock, darlin'?"

Jill released the tip of Dale's length. "Yeah, Dale—" Jill paused, unable to form words. She wanted Travis. Wanted him to pound into her. Wanted to clench around his thickness. "I-I want to come."

"Go for it, Trav."

Travis's calloused fingers grazed her clit, and she burst, soaring higher than the first climax.

Travis continued to thrust, and Dale soothed her with sexy words, how hot she was, how beautiful, how hard she made him. She absorbed it all in a heady rush.

When her release subsided, Travis pulled out of her, his cock still rock-hard, and disposed of his condom.

"Your turn, bud," he said to Dale. "And my turn to feel those gorgeous pink lips around my cock."

"Do you want that?" Dale asked Jill. "Do you want me to fuck you while you blow Travis?"

"Mmm, yes." More than anything, she wanted Dale's cock inside her. She wanted to force every last drop of cum out of him. And sucking Travis didn't sound too bad, either.

Dale leaned down and kissed her, slowly and passionately, and then flipped her over onto her tummy. "On your hands and knees, darlin'. I'm takin' you from behind." Dale fumbled with a condom, and soon his length teased the cheeks of her ass.

Travis knelt in front of her, his cock weeping with pre-cum. She grabbed his taut butt for support and licked the salty drops from him.

Meanwhile, Dale kissed her thighs, nipping and licking,

and tongued her pussy. "Mmm. You taste so good, Jill. Just like honeyed cream." He slid his tongue over her labia, and up over her anus.

Her tight hole puckered, and she shivered. Would he take her ass tonight? Would she let him?

★ ★ ★ ★

Travis reached for the pitcher of lemonade and poured some over his cock. "I want it to taste good for you, sweetheart."

His beautiful sex tasted just fine to Jill, but the lemonade added an extra zest that made it even better. She teased his cock head, licking around the sensitive rim and underside, and then took him a little farther. She slurped every drop of that mouthwatering beverage from him. And she enjoyed every minute.

"She gives great head, Trav," Dale said as he inserted a thick finger into her cunt.

Her walls pulsed around him.

"So tight, darlin'," he said. "I need to fuck you right now." He thrust into her wet channel, and his balls slapped against her clit. He plunged deep once, twice, and then once more.

Jill was on the verge of another breath-stealing climax. She grabbed Travis's ass and took his cock into her mouth again. She sucked him deep into her throat, his moans igniting her to take him even farther.

"Sweetheart, that's amazing," Travis said. "Absolutely amazing."

"Told you, Trav," Dale said, his words breathless. "Damn, you're tight, Jill. So tight and sweet. I love fuckin' you."

Jill wanted to answer, to tell Dale she loved fucking him

too, but her mouth was full of cock. She moaned, grinding back against Dale's thrusts. She felt so full, so well pleasured, and neither Travis nor Dale had released yet. The night was still young.

Dale continued to pound into her as she blew Travis. When the pad of his finger pushed against her anus, she trembled.

"Okay?" Dale rasped.

She released Travis's cock to answer. "Yeah, cowboy. Go ahead."

The cool sensation of lubricant, coupled with the heat of Dale's fingers, melted against Jill's tender flesh. He massaged her tight rim, and inserted his wet finger slowly, stretching her. The feeling was so invasive, so intense, but she relaxed into it, and found pleasure in having Dale fill her so thoroughly.

Travis's cock still dangled in front of her, but she leaned back into Dale's body and quivered as he added another finger and fucked her in two places at once. The climax took her by surprise. He hadn't even been touching her clit, but she shattered, and tiny sparks erupted on her flesh. She soared higher and higher, and her only regret was that Dale wasn't coming with her. She cried his name, her voice not quite her own.

"That's right, darlin'," he said. "Come. Come for me. Only for me."

Only for me. Had Dale forgotten Travis was there? Once her pussy relaxed, Dale removed his cock and pulled her against his chest in a tight embrace.

"That was phenomenal, Jill," he said. "Like nothing I've ever felt before."

"But you didn't—"

"No, not yet." He cupped her cheeks and pressed his lips softly to hers. "What was phenomenal was making you come like that. I loved it."

"But I want you to come. So far, this night's been all about me."

He chuckled against her lips. "All about you? I've had a rippin' good time. And so has Trav. Haven't you?"

"Hell, yeah. Watching you, and being a part of it, boggles my mind."

"You want to come some more, darlin'?" Dale kissed her cheek.

"I...I..."

"I'll take that as a yes." Dale's husky laugh vibrated against her neck. "Let's get you cleaned off. The hot tub's all fired up."

He stood and lifted Jill, and she wrapped her legs around his waist. Amazing, how their two bodies fit together, as though they'd been created for each other. Skin-to-skin with Dale was the most erotic, delicious and sweet sensation she'd ever felt.

"Come on, Trav," he said.

★ ★ ★ ★

Dale kept his hot tub lukewarm. That's how he and Jill preferred it. They could stay in as long as they wanted without getting overheated. Still, to prevent dehydration, he kept plenty of water handy. And another pitcher of honey-lemonade.

The warm water swished around his body, tickling him. His erection still raged. He could have come. He would have gotten hard again right away. Jill had that effect on him. He could fuck her every night for the rest of his life and not get tired of her beautiful body, her tight pussy, her amazing selfless heart.

God, he loved her.

The words he'd never said to a woman didn't particularly surprise him. Even though he hadn't formed them until now, they saturated his mind, as if they'd always been there and always would be. He loved Jill.

She sat on the edge of the hot tub, her legs spread, Travis's blond head bobbing between them. Her eyes were closed, and her body glistened with shiny perspiration in the moonlight. Sexy little moans escaped her throat.

She was beautiful. So fucking beautiful. And now, as he watched his best friend eat his woman's pussy, he knew, without a doubt, he'd spend the rest of his life with her.

Tonight was a gift. A gift she deserved, and he was glad to have given it. An experience she wouldn't soon forget.

But it wouldn't happen again. Jillian Reynolds would be his, and his alone, for eternity.

He tapped Travis's shoulder impatiently. "My turn."

Travis lifted his head, his chin gleaming with Jill's sweet cream. "Sure, bud." He moved to the other side of the tub.

Dale buried his face between the legs of the woman he loved. She smelled like peaches. Peaches, lemons, honey, and Jill. An inebriating combination, and one he wouldn't tire of any time soon. Slowly, he licked her slick folds, like silk against his tongue.

"Ah, Dale." She sighed. "I love when you lick me."

He groaned into her, taking her swollen labia between his teeth and tugging. She squealed. God, he loved sucking her, making her feel good. He knew just what she liked, and he lived for her moans, her sweet cries of ecstasy.

Between his legs, his cock throbbed. He'd been close to

release several times already, but he held off for her. He wanted to give her everything tonight. The ultimate pleasure. He sank his tongue into her moist slit. Nectar drenched his mouth and chin. He lapped her thoroughly, tensing his tongue and fucking her as deeply as he could. Then he pushed her thighs up toward her chest, careful so she wouldn't lose her balance on the edge, and licked her puckered anus.

"Dale!" she cried.

"Mmm. Good, darlin'?"

"The best." He released her thighs and nipped the inside of one. "I'm gonna take you there tonight."

"Mmm. I know." She inhaled, her beautiful breasts bobbing lightly against her chest. "I know."

"First, I want you to come again, though," he said, and then tongued her clit. "I want you to come. Then I want you to let Travis fuck your tight pussy again. Would you like that?"

"Mmm. Anything for you, Dale."

"It's all for you, darlin'. Only if it's what you want."

"It's...it's what I want."

"Then come," he rasped, his tone commanding, "come for me, Jill."

Dale thrust two fingers into her wet channel and sucked her clit hard. She shattered, her walls clenching around him as he massaged her G-spot, and fresh cream drizzled over his hand.

When her spasms slowed, he removed his fingers and pulled her into the warm water. He sat down on the bench, the water coming midway up his chest, and pulled Jill onto his lap.

"I want you to slide your clit up and down my hard cock, darlin', while Trav fucks you. Would you like that?"

"God, yes," she said.

Travis, condom already in place, moved behind Jill.

She didn't know it yet, but this was the last time she'd fuck another man. One last gift to her, to be sandwiched between two men, the object of both their desires. A jolt of jealousy speared into him and shattered his resolve for a moment. But he inhaled, gripped Jill's slippery body, and willed to give her this satisfaction one last time.

She sighed, soft and feathery against his neck, when Travis entered her.

"You have the tightest little pussy," Travis said, his face twisted into a grimace.

"Yeah, she sure does," Dale agreed. "Enjoy it." *For the last time.*

Jill slithered up and down Dale's shaft as Travis fucked her from behind. Dale was so hard he thought he'd explode if he didn't get to come soon. She was so beautiful. Her auburn ringlets, moist from the exertion and the steam from the tub, framed her pretty round face. Tiny beads of water dripped from the strands. A delectable strawberry hue flushed her cheeks, and her lips—those soft, sweet lips—were as red as a ruby.

Dale cupped her silky pink cheeks and drew her mouth to his for a kiss. A searing kiss that thundered through him. Jill's mouth was sweet as cherry wine. He thrust his tongue inside, sweeping it in the satiny warmth, branding her. It was a possessive kiss. A kiss that said, *you're mine. Another man may be fucking you, but you're mine. Now and forever.*

Jill's delicate sighs echoed with a soft vibration into Dale's mouth. Her clit sliding up and down his cock was sweet torture.

Behind her, Travis grunted, his face flushed. "Dale," he

gasped. "I can't hold off any longer. I have to come."

A ribbon of possessive lust knifed through Dale at his friend's words. This was Travis. His buddy. He loved him like a brother. Loved him enough to let him pleasure his woman. But it was over now.

Dale ripped his mouth away from Jill's and inhaled a much needed breath. "No."

"No?" Travis groaned as he pounded into Jill's pussy. "What do you mean?"

"I mean no. You don't come inside her."

"It's okay, bud. You know I'm wearing a raincoat."

"It's not okay. I don't want you to come inside her. Pull out and finish yourself off."

Travis's gaze met his, and Dale knew his friend understood. Travis withdrew, pulled off the condom, tossed it on the edge of the tub, and squeezed his eyes shut as he gripped his cock. Thick streams of cream spurted into his other hand. When he was finished, he wiped his hands on a towel sitting on the edge of the tub and then plunked down onto the lounge seat with a heavy sigh and a splash. He closed his eyes.

Jill's face was buried in Dale's neck, her moist body clamped to his. She hadn't watched Travis get off, which intrigued Dale.

"Darlin'?"

"Hmm?" Her voice hummed against Dale's earlobe.

"Are you ready?"

"Yes, Dale."

"You know what I'm talkin' about, don't you?"

"Yeah."

The soft flutter of her lips against his neck as she smiled warmed him.

"I know. And I'm ready." She lifted her head and her flushed face had never looked more beautiful.

He stood and helped her up. Without any prompting, she turned her back to him and braced her arms on the edge of the tub. So beautiful. Tiny droplets of moisture meandered down the swell of her round cheeks. So trusting, to give herself to him like this, and in front of his friend. At that moment, he loved her with an intensity he hadn't known existed.

"Jill." His own voice had deepened.

"Yes?"

"This is something I only want to share with you."

She nodded and wiggled her bottom against his erection.

Did she understand what he meant? He wasn't sure. His original plan had been to initiate her ass while Travis fucked her pussy. To let her be filled in the ultimate way. Previously, when he and Travis had pleasured women in this manner, Dale had always taken the pussy. Now, as he readied to make love to his woman in a new and exciting way, he yearned for oneness with her, and only her. Travis could watch, but the act was for Dale and Jill alone. He cleared his throat.

She twisted her neck around and met his gaze with her emerald eyes. "What is it?"

"I know you're a virgin here."

She nodded.

"What I mean is...I am too. I've never had anal sex. This is something I've saved for someone special. And I want that someone special to be you."

"Oh, Dale. Thank you."

Her smile dazzled him, and he bent to press a chaste kiss to her lips. He pushed the head of his cock into the soft valley between her butt cheeks and slid it up and down. Her little moans excited him.

He looked over his shoulder. Travis was gone. Dale smiled. His friend had decided to give them some privacy. He was the ultimate good guy.

Dale let his dick rest against the soft flesh of Jill's cheek as he reached for a tube of lubricant he had set next to the tub earlier. He squeezed a generous amount into his palm and smeared it over her anus. He worked one finger in, and then another, relishing the firmness of her muscles. Damn, this was going to feel good. With his free hand, he reached around the front of her and teased her clit. When he'd added a third finger, and a gush of nectar from her pussy coated his other hand, the time had come to make her his.

★ ★ ★ ★

Jill undulated against Dale's invading fingers. The invasive pain morphed into pleasure, and she found herself both desiring and fearing his cock. But the warmth from his confession—that he'd never shared this with another—gave her courage. Though she'd given up her vaginal virginity long ago, she could give this virginity to the man she loved. The man she hoped to spend the rest of her life with.

Hope speared through her. She'd know soon enough whether she'd be turning down that new job.

He pressed moist kisses to her dripping neck. "Darlin'."

"Yes?"

"I think you're ready."

She nodded. As ready as she could ever be. Ready for her man to take her.

"Don't worry, I'll go slow."

She nodded again, and the rip of a condom packet zinged in her ears. Cool lubricant coated her, and a few seconds later, the head of his cock nudged her anus. He pushed in, stretching her, and she winced at the sharpness.

"Easy, darlin'," he rasped against her neck. "I don't want to hurt you. You tell me if I need to stop."

No. She'd give him this gift. She wanted it as much as he did. And after what he'd given her tonight—the joy of being pleasured by two hot men—she wanted to give him something equally precious. Within a few seconds, she adjusted. "Go ahead, Dale. I want this."

"Ah, Jill." He inched in a little farther.

Not so bad this time. When his fingers found her clit, she relaxed and backed into him, taking him deeper.

"Darlin', that's nice," he said, his voice deep and husky.

She backed into him again, taking more of his enormous cock, and found that the fullness completed her in a primal yet soul-wrenching, way.

"That's it, take all of me."

Dale thrust into her ass, and when his balls slapped against her pussy, she knew he was part of her. And that he would be forever.

"Darlin', I want you so much," he said. "Tell me when you're ready."

So sweet to think of her, when he no doubt wanted to pound into her with a vengeance. They'd been going at it for hours, and he hadn't come yet. She wiggled against him, the intrusion of his cock in her tight tunnel a shocking, surprising pleasure. No longer uncomfortable, she found the fullness exciting. Was it pleasure because it felt good? Or was it pleasure because it was Dale inside her? In a place he'd never been with another woman, and she'd never been with another man?

Warmth exploded through her veins. Her blood boiled beneath her flesh. At that moment, she'd never wanted a man more. "I'm ready, Dale."

He pulled out and thrust in, and shivers rippled through her pussy. A soft sigh left her throat.

"Okay?" he asked.

"Mmm. Better than okay. Take me, cowboy. Take me to where neither of us has ever been. I want to go. With you."

"My sweet Jill." He plunged into her again.

Waves of joy sparked between her legs and threaded outward to every cell in her body. She met him thrust for thrust, taking all he gave her and relishing the carnal baseness of it. So good. Dale's fingers worked her clit as he penetrated her, and moisture drizzled down her inner thighs. Swirls of steam surrounded them, and beads of sweat trickled down her cheeks and neck.

Dale's other hand found a breast and cupped it, squeezed it, plucked at her hard nipple. The sensation—the amazing sensation—rainbowed over her flesh, through her blood, all the way to her heart.

And she exploded into the most earth-shattering climax she'd ever known.

Icy-hot spasms shook the walls of her pussy and ribboned through the rest of her body, culminating in sweet chills that rippled across her tingling skin. So intense was this joining, that for one glorious moment, their bodies and hearts seemed fused as one.

"That's right, darlin'," Dale's voice cut through the fog of her desire as her climax slowed, "come for me. Only for me."

Only for me. He gripped her hips and thrust one last time

into her, his slick body covering hers as he released. His cock pulsed into her tightness, and she backed into him again, wanting to give him everything she had. Everything she was.

Vibrant images and half-formed thoughts jumbled inside her head, a mass of feelings she couldn't quite string together in any coherent way. But three words forced their way to the top of the heap.

I love you.

How she longed to utter them. And to hear Dale say them back. Maybe sometime soon.

Dale was still buried deep within her. "Ah, Jill." He panted against her neck. "This meant so much to me."

"Me too." Truer words had never left her lips. Tears stung the corners of her eyes.

He slid out of her, and she turned to face his deep, dark eyes. So gorgeous. His handsome face was shiny with perspiration, threads of nearly black hair stuck to his cheeks. Droplets trickled along the chiseled angles of his cheeks, nose, and chin. His night beard had surfaced and caught drips of moisture. He'd never looked better.

She pressed her body against his in a fierce hug. She slid her slick breasts against his dampened chest hair, and her nipples pebbled. She'd never get enough of this man. Oh, to be alone with the one she loved...

Alone? She jerked away. Where had Travis gone? "Dale?"

"Hmm?"

"Where's Travis?"

Dale pulled her back into his embrace and chuckled against her cheek. "He must've gone inside. Probably wanted to give us a little privacy. And I don't know about you, but I appreciated it."

She smiled against his beefy shoulder. "Me too."

Dale lifted her, easing his hands under her slick bottom, and set her on the edge of the hot tub. He quickly disposed of the condom. "You thirsty, darlin'?"

She was. Ravenously so. "After that? You bet."

He reached for the lemonade and handed it to her. She took a long drink straight from the pitcher. The crisp citrus flavor flowed down her throat like nectar from the gods. After a couple more swills, she handed the pitcher back to Dale. "Here, you must be thirsty too." She grinned. "Have I ever told you how much I love your homemade honey-lemonade?"

His lazy grin lit up his handsome face. "A few times." He downed several swallows of the beverage. Still holding the pitcher, he helped her to her feet. "You want to go inside?"

Inside? Travis would be there. And though she liked the other man, she kind of wanted to be alone with Dale for the rest of the night. But they couldn't be rude to his guest. "Sure. Let's go on in."

Dale wrapped her wet body in a fluffy towel and led her across the redwood deck to the sliding glass doors. The house was dark.

Dale flipped the light switch in the kitchen. "Trav?" he called out.

No response.

"Maybe he had to leave," Jill said.

"Hmm. That's not like him to just up and disappear."

Jill walked around the kitchen and turned on another light. A folded piece of paper addressed to Dale and her sat on the counter. She picked it up and ran her wrinkled fingers along the crease. "Dale? I think he left us a note."

Dale came up behind her. "Go ahead and read it, darlin'."

"I wouldn't feel right. He's your friend."

"I think you're as close to him as I am now." He smiled and chucked her under the chin.

"Still—" She handed the paper to Dale.

"Okay." He unfolded the note and glanced over it.

Jill's skin chilled a little. She wasn't sure why. "What is it?"

He grinned. "Nothing. Here"—he handed her the letter—"you can read it."

Jill took the crisp white paper.

Dale and Jill,

Thank you for tonight. I've never experienced anything quite so intense, and I won't forget it. You two have something really special together. Don't let it get away. Hope to see you both again soon. I'll call you when I'm back in town, Dale. And Jill, it was a true pleasure to make love to you, one I know Dale won't grant me again. Don't ask me how I know. He'll tell you when he's ready.

Fondly, Travis

Jill's pulse raced like a hummingbird's wings. Her skin heated. "Dale?"

"Hmm?"

"Is that true? You won't let him make love to me again?"

He cupped her cheek. "Oh yeah, darlin'. That is so fuckin' true."

"Why?" Jill's heart thudded. "I thought you and Travis liked to give a woman the pleasure of two men."

"Yes, I can't deny that. But it's past tense for me now."

"Oh?"

He smiled. "God, I hope you feel the same way."

"Well sure. I enjoyed tonight, but if you don't want to do it again, I'm okay with that."

"Good." He fingered her moist curls. "You're so beautiful."

Emotion tugged at her tummy. "Thank you."

"I wanted to give you tonight. It was for you. An experience you deserved to have. And it was your only chance to have it."

"It was?"

"Sure as hell was, if I have anything to say about it." His bronze eyes burned into hers. "Do I, Jill?"

Desire swept through her, laced with a touch of confusion. What exactly was he saying? "Do you what?"

"Have anything to say about it."

"If you have something to say, Dale, I sure wish you'd just say it."

"Okay." He cleared his throat and seared her with his smoldering eyes. "I won't share you again. I want you to be mine and only mine."

She launched herself into his arms. Happiness—pure, unadulterated joy—surged through her. "I'm yours," she said. "I'm yours, Dale. I didn't need tonight."

"You mean you didn't enjoy it?"

"Oh, I enjoyed it. It was a pure physical pleasure. But with you, Dale, I get more. We came together tonight on a level that was way more than physical."

"Ah, God." He rained kisses across her cheeks before clamping his mouth to hers.

The kiss spoke of passion. Of possession.

Of love.

When he released her, he cupped her face and gazed into her eyes. "I love you. Do you know that?"

She nodded, and a lone tear trickled down her cheek. "I love you too, Dale. I have for a while now."

He brushed the tear away. "Don't cry, darlin'." Then a grin split his face from ear to ear. "Damn, woman, why didn't you tell me?"

"Why didn't you tell me?"

"Because I'm an idiot." He laughed. "It took ol' Trav."

"I suppose he knew what he was doing."

"Hell, he might have had an inkling, but he also wanted to get in your pants. And I can't say as I blame him. I'm thinkin' the same thing right about now."

"Yeah?" Her body responded with chilled skin, a heated pussy. Moisture dribbled between her legs. Mere words from Dale could turn her on. "After the night we just had, you're ready for more?"

"With you? Always." He seared her lips with his.

Her hands crept over his muscled chest. She fingered his hard nipples and then rested her hand over his heart. It beat in synchrony with her own.

When he broke the kiss, he wrenched the towel from her body and slid his fingers into her slick folds. "Mmm. So wet for me. Already so wet."

She quivered at his touch, and then removed the terry towel from around his waist. His cock stood at attention— hard, long and magnificent. She dropped to her knees and flicked her tongue over the salty head.

"Wet," she echoed. "That's exactly how I'm going to give it to you, cowboy. The way you like it. Slow and wet."

Primal Instinct

PRIMAL INSTINCT

The scent was unmistakably male.

Two bodies crushed hard against her while Erin leaned against the bar, waiting for the bartender. She had planned to spend most of the week hiding away in the small cabin she'd rented in the Rocky Mountains, but after two days of seclusion, she visited the clubhouse of the rustic resort for a drink.

She breathed in the spicy aroma. Beach. Leather. A touch of cinnamon. Undeniable male musk. Primal.

A year of involuntary celibacy—were all thirty-something men married, gay, or brainless boobs?—had prompted Erin to take a week of vacation and embark on a soul-searching pilgrimage.

Men. Who needed them? She'd get to know herself. Get to know what made Erin Monroe tick and contemplate a life of single solitude.

The enticing virile fragrance, not to mention the warmth of two hot bodies, wasn't helping her cause.

"Can I help you?" the bartender asked.

Erin's skin prickled. She looked to her left, and then to her right. Four slightly slanted masculine eyes—two blue and clear, two dark and smoky—burned into her.

"She'll have what we're having," the dark-eyed man said.

She turned. "Excuse me?" A mug of stout sat in front of him. "I don't drink beer. So no, thank you."

"Whatever you want then, honey," he said. "It's on us."

"For sure," Blue Eyes said.

He edged his body closer to hers, until not a part of her wasn't touching him. Erin tingled. What the hell was going on? The invasion seemed far too intimate, though they were all fully clothed and in a public place.

She warmed with embarrassment over how she was dressed. Sweats and a tank top. Clingy, yes, and her body was pretty good thanks to daily yoga. But sweats? She was hardly clothed to socialize. Even less to pick up men. The two men, though, looked gorgeous in loose faded jeans. Dark Eyes wore a black polo, Blue Eyes a faded gray T-shirt. Both sported finely sculpted shoulders and arms. How might they feel beneath her fingertips?

Remember the purpose of this self-imposed mini-retreat. Be strong, Erin.

"What's your name, beautiful?" Blue Eyes drew his words out almost like a purr. His long finger drifted over her hand on the bar.

Erin edged her hand away from his warmth. A sense of loss washed over her. She ignored his question and faced the woman tending bar. "A gin and tonic, please." She fumbled in her handbag for money.

Blue Eyes threw a twenty onto the counter. "Keep the change," he said.

Erin extended her hand to reach for the bill before the bartender took it.

Blue Eyes covered her hand with his. "Please, let us."

A spark shot through Erin at the contact. "But I don't even know you."

"You will, as soon as you tell us your name."

Erin's heart sped up at the man's gorgeous smile. He

was blond and perfect, and the warmth from his hand on hers spread to every cell in her body. Her skin blazed.

"I'm Landon Kay," he said, "and this is my...friend, Nick Foster."

She turned and gazed into Nick's dark eyes.

"Pleasure." Nick reached for her other hand and brushed his full lips lightly across her fingertips.

Nick was dark where Landon was fair. Two incredibly perfect males. Two incredibly perfect bodies on either side of her. Her blood sizzled and her heart thumped.

Nick dropped her hand and traced one warm finger across her cheek. A low hum resonated. His voice, just like Landon's. A purr. "Tell us your name, honey."

"Erin," she said without meaning to. "Erin Monroe."

"Mmm." From behind, Landon purred into her neck.

Shivers raced through her and landed between her legs.

★ ★ ★ ★

Erin wasn't sure how she ended up in their cabin. She'd left her drink sitting untouched on the bar, so she couldn't blame the alcohol. Hell, one drink wouldn't have impaired her judgment anyway. She'd followed them as if in a trance.

Both men rubbed up against her, Nick in front, Landon behind, their bodies hard and ready. She should have been frightened. Freaked.

She wasn't.

"You're beautiful." Landon pulled the band holding her brown hair in a ponytail and let her tresses sift through his fingers. "Like silk," he said. "Mahogany silk." He inhaled. "Apples. Tart apples."

Nick smoothed the strap of her tank top off her shoulder and dropped a light kiss onto her bare skin. The soft whisper of his lips made her quiver.

"Apples," Nick echoed. "You sure it's her hair, Lan?" His lips curved against her flesh.

Fresh juice trickled between her thighs. Her panties would be soaked by now. What was she doing here with not one, but two men? Two *strange* men?

"No." Landon brushed his lips against Erin's cheek. "I wasn't talking about her hair." He kissed her nose, her other cheek. "I was talking about her sweet juicy cunt."

Her breath caught. The c-word. Instead of horrifying her, the word made her hot. "What am I doing here?"

"Oh, honey," Nick said, "you're doing what you were put on earth to do."

"And that is?" Her voice cracked.

"Making love to us." Nick's hand slid up her waist and cupped one breast. He groaned. "Both of us."

"You can't mean..."

"Oh, yes we can." Landon cupped the other breast. "And we do."

"But shouldn't we..." What had she meant to say?

"Get to know each other?" Landon chuckled into her hair. "We will. Don't you worry."

Erin fell limp between their two beautiful bodies. How had Landon known what she meant? She looked into his sparkling azure eyes. Though tall herself, these men dwarfed her, both six-four at least. She stood, paralyzed, aching to touch them, to sift her fingers through Nick's dark locks, Landon's blond waves. Nick's broad and beefy shoulders beckoned. The golden curls peeking from the V of Landon's T-shirt begged to be caressed.

"Go ahead," Landon said, reading her mind again.

"Yes," Nick purred. "Touch us. We want you to touch us."

"You're the most beautiful woman we've ever seen." Landon pushed against her, his erection apparent at her side.

The most beautiful woman *we've* ever seen. They talked as one. Strange.

And strangely arousing.

Emotion, thick and heady, coursed through her. Her body was ready, no doubt, but her mind? Her heart? Why did this seem so normal? So right?

Shaking, she cupped Nick's chiseled cheek. His smile warmed her, and his stubble scraped her palm.

"Your eyes are the color of pine trees in the moonlight."

Erin's nipples tightened. Her eyes were a dull greenish gray. Nick made them sound glorious.

But glorious they were not. Her heart thudded to her stomach. This had to stop. Now. No way was she going to have a threesome with two strangers, no matter how wet she was for them. She opened her mouth to say as much, but Nick's lips covered hers.

The kiss was crushing, almost violent. He ate at her lips, bit them, sucked them, and then sank his tongue between them and devoured her mouth. His erection throbbed against her belly, and another, Landon's, pressed into her back. Tiny nibbles trailed over the sensitive skin of her neck. Landon. The throaty rumbles of their groans vibrated around her.

These men wanted her. Why? She hadn't a clue, but at this moment, with her nipples straining and her pussy pulsing, she couldn't bring herself to care. Mini-retreat be damned.

She was going to do this. She had no choice. Her body had

taken over. She would make love to two flawless men. Even better, they were going to make love to *her*.

Nick's nimble fingers eased her tank up her chest, and Landon unclasped her bra in back. Her breasts fell gently against her hot skin. Landon cupped them from behind and gently plucked at her turgid nipples, all the while grinding his hardness into the small of her back.

Nick ripped his mouth from hers and covered Landon's hands with his own. "Damn, you've got great nipples. Pink as a mountain sunrise. Just the right size to suck on."

Erin shivered as he bent to one.

"You're going to need to move your fingers, Lan."

"Aw..." Landon eased her sweats over her hips and massaged the crease between her ass cheeks. "Good thing there are other things for me to do."

Her blood boiled. From Landon massaging her ass? Or from Nick nibbling on her nipple? Or simply from being sandwiched between two beautiful men? She closed her eyes and inhaled.

At this rate, she'd be a puddle of honey on the floor before long.

"Oh!" Make that now. Puddle on the floor. Landon's long finger found her wetness and drilled into her pussy.

"Tight," he purred, "and wet. Feels so good around my finger." He inhaled against her neck. "And you smell like tart apple pie. Damn, I can't wait to taste you."

"Mmm." Nick's breath whispered against the swollen flesh of her breast. "Cut you a deal. You taste her first. I get to fuck her first."

Erin caressed Nick's granite shoulders. A soft moan left her throat.

"You like that, honey?" Nick rasped against her nipple. "You like Lan to rub your hot little clit and finger fuck you?"

"Yes." The word was more breath than speech.

"Wait till I stuff your pussy with my cock." He left her breasts and stood tall, leaning to whisper in her ear. "I'm going to make you scream."

Red heat whirled around her. So hot in this room. So very hot.

Still, this situation... She had every intention of following through. To hell with her mini-retreat. Her body was on fire. But she needed to know more. "You guys, I need to know why you're doing this. Why you...together..."

"Shh." Nick traced the outer shell of her ear with his hot tongue. "We'll explain it all later. Now is the time for pleasure."

"But—"

"You just concentrate on us. Feel Lan's fingers sliding in and out of you. Think about me shoving my dick into you. I'm so hard right now. I'm going to fuck you soon, Erin Monroe."

"And when he's done"—Landon's warm breath caressed her shoulder—"I'm going to take you. Ram my cock into you until you don't know your own name."

Erin. Her name was Erin. Beyond that she couldn't remember much.

"We're not easy lovers," Landon continued. "We're going to take you hard. And you're going to enjoy every heart-pounding, breath-stealing minute of it."

Oh, hell, yeah. She would. Landon's hard body glided down her back. He slid her sweats and panties the rest of the way down her legs. His teeth grazed her ass cheeks, and his hands whispered along her inner thighs.

"Step out of your flip-flops, sweet."

She obeyed, and he tossed the shoes and the discarded sweats onto a nearby chair. At least she thought he did. Nick had gone back to nibbling her nipples, so her brain was mush.

"Gorgeous long legs." Landon's warm breath drifted into the crease of her ass. "Fucking beautiful ass. You know what that means, don't you, Nick?"

"You want the ass first?"

"It's only fair. You get that sweet pussy first."

The ass? Were they kidding? "Uh, guys..."

"Shh," Nick murmured against her breast. "You'll love it."

Love it? She might. The idea had merit. Right now, though, she really wanted Landon's fingers in her pussy again. "Landon?"

He shoved them into her and tongued her anus at the same time.

"Damn." Oh, she'd shatter in a minute. If only she could reach her clit. She inched her fingers downward. "Do you read minds?"

Landon slurped a wet kiss between her cheeks. "Only yours."

"God."

Nick released her nipple with a soft smack. "The bed, Lan. She's not going to be able to stand much longer."

Now *Nick* was reading her mind. How was any of this possible?

"Mmm. The bed sounds good." Landon gripped her hips with firm hands. "As much as I like tonguing your sweet little asshole, I really want to sink into that luscious pussy."

Nick seared her flesh with smoky dark eyes. "And as soon as he sucks you till you're swollen as a new peach, I'm going to slam my cock into you."

Shivers skittered across Erin's skin. Nick was no longer purring. His voice was raw, untamed. He was growling. Growling like an animal.

What a fucking turn-on. Not easy lovers, Landon had said. Primal instinct swirled around her so thick she swore she could feel it massaging her skin. They were going to fuck her like animals.

She couldn't wait.

"I'm gonna make her come first." Landon.

"I'm gonna make her come harder." Nick.

Clearly, they both liked control. Yeah, she was okay with that. But for now, she had something to say before they robbed her of her ability to speak altogether.

"I'll be happy to come as many times as the two of you can manage." Her voice was low and sultry. Since when had she become a seductress? "But I won't until we take care of one tiny detail."

Nick bit her areola. The pleasure-pain hit her between the legs. No, damn it. She wouldn't come yet.

"What detail?" Nick hummed against her throbbing breast.

"You two"—she inhaled a much-needed breath—"need to strip." She dug her heels into the plush carpet. "Now."

Erin's heart hammered as they revealed two perfect male bodies. Nick, with dark hair scattered across a sculpted chest and a magnificent cock jutting from black curls. Landon, whose chest hair was blond and whose cock was just as regal in its golden nest. Two gorgeous sets of flawless pecs and abs. Both of similar height, with strong legs and arms. So unequaled, they could have been sculpted by a Renaissance artist.

Moisture trickled between her thighs. These two dazzling

men were really going to make love to her.

She lay down on the bed and those two hard bodies pressed into her from either side. Touching. They liked touching. She'd be happy to oblige.

"Spread your legs, Erin." Landon's breath feathered across her swollen breasts as he inched down her body, the warmth of his skin never leaving hers. He entwined his thick fingers in her brown curls and inhaled.

"Apples, Erin. You have no idea how much I love a fresh, crispy apple." His fingers slid through her folds. "So wet, baby. So fucking wet."

Oh, yeah. She was wet all right. Landon's fingers thrust harder and harder, finding a spot that made her convulse. When the moist tip of his tongue probed her clit, a climax hit her full force. Vibrations shimmied through her body, but before ecstasy had barely waned, Nick had straddled her chest and the head of his cock prodded against her lips.

"You turn an adorable shade of pink when you come, honey." He nudged his cock head into her mouth. "Wait till *I* make you come, though. It'll be fucking fantastic."

No doubt it would be. Erin took Nick's shaft between her lips. A drop of pre-cum salted her tongue. She licked the smooth tip, his groans exciting her.

All the while Landon worked her pussy like a cat lapping rich cream. Strong hands pushed her thighs upward. Her pussy was at Landon's mercy. His lips, teeth, and tongue tantalized her labia, her slick opening, and especially her swollen clit. Her whole body hummed with awareness. Warmth, and then cold. Then warmth again. She writhed, ground her cunt against Landon's talented mouth. Taking more of Nick's engorged cock, she sucked and released, the thrusts of her lips in tandem with her hips as Landon stabbed her with his long, sleek tongue.

"Mmm," he said against her wetness. "You taste so good, baby. I could eat you all night."

Nick increased the thrusts of his hips, giving her more cock. Happy to oblige, she sucked him deep, his tip grazing the back of her throat. What she wouldn't give to suck him to completion, to feel the warmth of his cum trickle into her mouth, down her throat.

"Sorry, honey." He withdrew. "Not this time. I'm coming in that sweet cunt of yours."

Again? How did he know what she was thinking?

Landon's finger plunged into her. God, she was going to come again. But she wanted Nick to come. She whimpered. She wanted to swallow his cum, taste his essence.

Glistening and beautiful, Nick's penis bobbed against her chin. She craned her neck, but he held it just out of her reach.

For a split second, Erin thought she might die if she couldn't taste his cum, but when a forceful climax hit her, all thoughts washed away.

Only feeling remained. Beautiful unbridled feeling. She soared, and her body shivered. Icy warmth glided through her, and when she relaxed, Nick was between her legs. Both he and Landon probed her pussy. Two thick fingers nursed her through the remains of her climax. Slow and sweet, they slid in and out.

"Mmm, beautiful, Erin," Nick said. "You're beautiful when you come."

"Yes, you are," Landon agreed. His finger drifted from her channel, leaving Nick penetrating her.

"Turn her over and take her from behind," Landon said. "I

want those luscious lips on my dick."

Nick slid his finger from her and gently rolled her to her tummy. "Gorgeous ass," he murmured. He slapped both cheeks lightly.

Never had Erin imagined a slap could feel so good. The sting reverberated through her body and landed back at her clit. Aching, throbbing. How could she still be so needy after two orgasms?

Oh, but she was. She needed more. So much more. Nick's cock in her pussy. Landon's in her mouth. That would be a good start. She wiggled her bottom and crawled up on her knees.

"Beautiful." Nick probed her pussy with his thick fingers and trailed the wetness into the crease of her ass. He pressed on her anus.

She jolted.

"Mmm, like that?"

Erin couldn't speak. She thought her head nodded, but she wasn't sure.

Gently, slowly, he poked the tip of his finger into her tight opening. Her tissues tensed and then relaxed, and tingles shot through her.

Landon sat at the head of the bed, his legs spread, giving Erin access to his beautiful cock and musky balls. She inhaled his pungent bouquet—spice and horny man. Intoxicating.

She glided her hips back and forth as Nick continued to drill her ass.

"Tight. So tight."

"Don't forget, Nick. I get first dibs on her ass."

"Just getting her ready for you."

When he slid his finger from her, Erin whimpered at the loss, but the knob of Landon's cock beckoned between her lips.

With Landon's hardness lodged firmly against the roof of her mouth, she felt the sweet nudge of Nick's cock head against her swollen folds.

He entered her with one smooth thrust. Ah, she hadn't known how achingly empty she was until she was filled. Nick penetrated her gently at first, and then increased his tempo to a fiery cadence that she transferred to the blow job she was giving Landon. She ate at his cock, savoring, relishing the joy of giving pleasure.

"Yeah, baby, just like that." Landon fisted his hands in her hair and pulled her more forcibly onto him. "Take me. Take all of me."

He grazed her throat, and as with Nick, she wished for him to come. To taste him.

Again, as with Nick, he wouldn't let her. He withdrew. "In your ass, baby. I'm coming in your ass."

And Nick pounded her. In and out. Such a heady joining. As though he were made for her, and she for him.

For them.

"Yeah, honey, yeah. So good. Made for me. For my cock." Nick's voice was low, raspy. Again, like a growl. "You fit me like a glove." He thrust deep. "Tell me you like it. Tell me you like it, Erin."

"I like it, Nick." She panted against Landon's hard thigh. "I love it."

Landon smoothed her moist hair away from her face. "Nick fucks you hard, doesn't he?"

She nodded, her forehead sliding against the moist tip of his cock.

"I'll fuck you just as hard, just as good. Maybe even better, baby."

Hard to imagine better than the commanding fucking she was getting. Her thighs quivered like jelly. She leaned down into Landon's balls. Her tongue crept out and licked them.

Thrust. Thrust. Thrust.

Nick fucked her deep. He ground into her, forcing her tunnel to take every last centimeter. And she was glad to do it. Glad to take all he had to give. Her tissues stretched to accommodate him. Slow fiery burn morphed into slick primal wanting.

Penetration. Sweet penetration. And then...more.

His finger glided into her ass.

She burst.

"Nick!" Her scream was muffled as she bit into Landon's muscled thigh. Swirls of heat kaleidoscoped through her. He hammered her as her pussy clenched around him. She relished each spasm, each contraction. Still, he pummeled into her. The more she came, the tighter she became, and she felt every vein on his magnificently sculpted cock as he filled her.

"That's it. Come for me." He worked another finger into her ass.

The exquisite stretch catapulted her into another climax.

She unclenched her teeth from Landon's thigh. He stroked her hair as she nibbled at his balls. Damn, he tasted good.

"Yeah, baby," he said. "Keep coming. Let it happen."

Ages later, as the convulsions slowed, Nick rammed into her with a final thrust.

"Ah, God!" he roared. "Just like that. Let me fill you. You hold me so tightly, Erin."

"Good girl," Landon said, caressing her cheek.

She tilted her head upward and met his blue gaze.

"And now it's my turn."

When Nick slipped from her pussy, Landon gathered her into her arms and kissed her. Like Nick's kiss, it was strong and possessive. Not an easy kiss. Lots of nibbling, lots of tongue. Her pussy throbbed to life again. Would she ever get enough of these two?

Hot, so hot. Yet she shivered in Landon's strong arms. She broke the kiss to take a needed breath.

"You can take more, right baby?" he whispered against her ear. His tongue slid along the outer shell.

She nodded. "I can take more. I want to take more."

Oh, how she wanted to take more.

Nick returned to the bed and took her from Landon's arms. "Lan will make sure you're ready. Don't worry. We'll make it good for you."

Nick laid her gently on her back and nuzzled her neck. "You'll love it, I promise."

Love what?

Oh. Her ass. Landon wanted to fuck her ass. She tensed.

Nick petted her. "It will be all right. You liked my finger, didn't you?"

"Yes." She had liked that. But a cock was a different matter altogether. Still, she wanted to do it. Wanted to be with Landon—with both of them—in that way. Why? She still wasn't sure. But she wanted it.

Landon spread her legs. His blond waves tickled her inner thighs. "Don't be afraid," he said. I'd never hurt you, Erin."

Somehow, she knew he spoke the truth.

He pushed her thighs forward gently and began to massage her anus. She jerked forward when something slippery and cool melted against her skin.

"Shh, baby." Landon's fingers slowly caressed her. "It's

just some lube to ease my entry. Make it more comfortable for you."

More comfortable. That was good.

"Let me help you," Nick said. He rained tiny kisses over the sensitive flesh of her neck, her breasts, and zeroed in on a hard nipple.

"Sugar nipples." He nibbled and tugged.

Sensation surged to her pussy. She loved to have her nipples sucked. They were so responsive, so sensitive, and Nick knew just how to drive her over the edge.

"I'm going to keep you so occupied," he rasped against her breast, "you won't feel any pain at all."

He licked her tight bud, slid his tongue in the valley between her breasts. Moist, warm. So good. A soft sigh escaped her throat.

Landon worked the lubricant into her opening, and when his finger breached her, she felt only pleasure. Soon he added another finger while Nick continued to tongue down her belly, dip into her navel, and trail up the outside of her thigh.

He brushed a wet kiss to her knee. "She's so beautiful, isn't she, Lan?"

Another finger plunged into her ass, and Erin tensed, but then relaxed when Nick's tongue went to work on her clit.

"Mmm. She sure is," Landon agreed. "Gorgeous red cunt, dripping with juice. Pretty pink asshole, so tight."

Nick's dark hair tickled her belly as he licked her clit ever so softly. Not enough to really get her going, but enough so her pussy clamored for more.

She writhed, trying to lift her hips. But she couldn't, not with her thighs in the air.

"Easy, baby." Landon lifted her bottom. "You're ready for

me now. I won't hurt you."

"I know you won't."

Nick held her hips in the air. She closed her eyes, expecting a stab of pain. But as Landon gripped her butt cheeks and his cock head nudged into her, she felt only the smallest twinge. He went slowly, as he'd promised, inch by inch, until he was embedded in her ass.

She opened her eyes and looked at his handsome face dotted with sweat. His blue eyes were closed, his teeth gritted together. "Landon?"

"I'm fine, baby. It just...feels...so...*good*."

Nick sucked her clit between his full firm lips. A jolt of pleasure ripped through her as Landon withdrew and plunged into her ass.

"Oh!" So full. Never been this full.

Nick's head remained between her legs. He licked her clit, nibbled it, sucked it, and forced a finger into her pussy and massaged her G-spot.

All the while Landon rocked into her ass with his impressive cock.

Rainbows. Skyrockets. Good God, this had to be nirvana. Two beautiful men between her legs. Total ecstasy.

Nick raised his head, and his dark gaze seared into hers as he continued to drill his finger into her wet sheath. "Let it go, honey. Feel it. Savor it. Let the lust consume you. Take you."

She looked to Landon, but his eyes were squeezed shut. Drops of perspiration beaded on his forehead and meandered down his cheeks, through his golden stubble.

Faster and harder he plundered her ass, and she loved it. Loved every nasty minute of it.

She turned back to Nick's sable eyes. *Let it go*, she heard in her mind. *Let it take you.*

Fragments of images blurred in her mind. Mountains. Streams. Nature. Animals frolicking, copulating. Majestic birds flying overhead. And in the middle of all of it, Nick and Landon pleasuring her. Taking her to the highest peak.

And a pleasure so fierce, so absolute, swept her away.

★ ★ ★ ★

Mmm. Sweet sleep. Erin woke and stretched, sighed again. Her body still sated from the glorious lovemaking, she leaned to the right, expecting to encounter a hard body.

Nothing but rumpled sheets on both sides. What? This hadn't been some sort of fantastic horny dream, had it? She widened her eyes and let them adjust to the darkness. Kitchen to the right, living area to the left. No. This wasn't her cabin. Hers had only a kitchenette and a bed.

Thank God. It hadn't been a figment of her imagination. But where were Nick and Landon? Why would they leave her alone in the cabin?

She wrapped a sheet around herself, stalked to the door, opened it, and stepped out into the moonlit night. The Rocky Mountains were beautiful. So majestic. Pine trees in the moonlight were a soft silvery green. Like her eyes.

She smiled as warmth enveloped her. Nick and Landon had made her feel beautiful. Beautiful and desirable. She hugged the sheet around her breasts.

Fresh mountain air stimulated her lungs. Deep and calming breaths soothed her, but again she wondered where the two men had gone. Never had a guy left her at his place.

Her body throbbed and ached. She yearned for these two

men who were still virtually strangers to her. They'd touched something inside her, something no one had ever touched. Something she didn't even know existed. Her soul.

They hadn't left her. But that didn't ease her curiosity about where they'd gone. She closed her eyes and breathed in the invigorating scent of pine once more. Mmm.

When a rustling met her ears, she opened her eyes. In the distance, two animals wrestled. Her heart lurched. Icy prickles stabbed into her neck. Were they mountain lions? Bears? Wolves? She squinted to see better as she backed toward the door of the cabin.

What? Her pulse skittered as she blinked.

Her eyes must be playing tricks on her.

The animals were lions. Two maned males. One a pale honey like the moonlight that shone on his coat, the other a deep tawny gold. Both wild and beautiful. Her heart thumped. When the pale one opened his mouth and a roar rocked the ground beneath her, she fled into the cabin and locked the door.

Perspiration dripped from her hairline as she thunked her body against the wood door.

Lions? In the Rockies? Surely she was seeing things. Mountain lions, yes, but these were true lions. The kind from Africa.

She closed her eyes and tried to steady her erratic breathing. No lions. Her eyes were bad. But her ears, too? She had heard that roar as sure as she could feel her own skin tingling, Bristling.

A loud knock on the door vibrated against her back.

"Erin?" Nick's voice.

"It's us, baby," Landon said. "Let us in."

Thank God. They'd protect her. She twisted the deadbolt

and jerked the door open. Her two lovers stood, stark naked, moonlight flowing across their sweat-glistened bodies.

She launched herself into them. Tears flowed from her eyes. "I am so glad to see you. Where have you been? I was frightened."

Four strong arms encircled her and two warm bodies nudged her through the entryway. Her men. Sparks and comfort simultaneously shot through her. Landon shut and bolted the door and hit the light switch while Nick continued to embrace her.

"You never have to be afraid again, Erin," he said. "Not while we're around."

His soothing words consoled her, sank right to her heart. She nuzzled his damp chest. "You're not going to believe this. I thought I saw lions outside."

Nick's voice rumbled against her ear. "Why wouldn't we believe you?"

"Because it's silly, that's why. There aren't any lions in Colorado. Other than mountain lions, I mean." She shook her head, and his chest hair tickled her cheek. "I...all that lovemaking must have made me a little crazy. I mean... It was amazing. I've never come so many times, so hard..."

Landon nudged into her from behind, his cock rigid against her back. "We'd believe just about anything," he whispered in her ear. His tongue tickled her lobe.

She shivered. So warm, so moist, their bodies slid against hers. Her pussy responded with an exquisite ache. She puckered her lips against Nick's chest and kissed him. His groan was her reward.

"Back to bed?" he asked.

"Mmm." Landon hummed against her ear. "Works for

me."

"Oh, yeah, works for me," Erin echoed. They nudged her toward the rumpled bed. "To think. Lions." She shook her head and giggled. "I've definitely lost it."

Nick nibbled at her neck. "I don't know. You'd be amazed what you can find up here in the mountains."

She laughed again. "Maybe. But lions? Impossible."

Landon purred against her shoulder and stroked it with his soft tongue. Heat flooded through her. Her breasts were still plastered against Nick's sweaty chest. She rubbed them against his nipples. Mmm, nice.

But a little clammy. Why were they both dripping with perspiration? And why had they been outside naked? Did it matter? That bed tempted. Beckoned...

Gathering all her willpower, she slid from between their bodies and stepped away from the bed. "I'd love nothing more than a repeat of our earlier fun, but I'm afraid I need some answers first."

Four smoking eyes bored into her. Neither asked what she wanted to know. Strange.

"What were you two doing outside in the middle of the night?"

"Taking a run," Landon said.

"Naked?"

Nick smiled. Oh, the dimples in those stubbled cheeks could melt steel. *Stick to your guns, Erin.*

"Yes, naked," Nick said. "We run naked. Together."

"Geez. You guys aren't—"

"No," Landon said. "We're both only concerned with your sexual pleasure."

He'd read her mind again. What was going on here? "Okay.

Can't you do your workout during the day?"

"Workout?" Landon's brows furrowed.

"Yeah, your running."

"We don't run for exercise," Nick said. "We run because we have to."

Erin let out a harsh sigh. Maybe it would be easier to just have hot monkey sex again. Who needed answers?

"She needs to know," Nick said to Landon.

"Later, Nick. I want to fuck her again."

Fucking? Sounded good to Erin. She inhaled their earthy masculine scent. It was more potent than before. More...robust. It tickled her nostrils, her senses, consumed her, streamed through her veins like hot lava. Her skin was suddenly warm, her pussy hot. Tiny spasms rocked through her clit. She wanted to fuck. Wanted to come. Now.

"No." Nick placed his palm on Landon's shoulder. "She needs to know. Can't you see? Look at her. Her skin is pink." He inhaled. "Her pussy's wet. Damn, she smells good." He inhaled again, eyes closed, and then opened them abruptly. "She's under the influence of our pheromones."

Under the influence? What the hell?

"She won't be sleeping with us of her own free will at this point. We need to tell her. Make her understand. Then when she comes to us, she'll know the truth."

Landon sighed. "Shit. You're right." He plunked down on the bed. "Baby, we need to talk."

Talk? Talking meant no fucking. Fucking was much better. Erin reached for Landon's erection.

He brushed her hand away. "Sorry, baby. Trust me, it's not that I don't want to."

Nick pulled a chair from the kitchen table and set it about

two feet from the bed. "Sit down, love."

Erin complied as Nick sat on the bed next to Landon. Their two cocks stood at attention. Her mind was a white haze. What was all this talking nonsense? She wanted cocks. In her hand, her mouth, her pussy, her ass. She trembled, burning for pleasure and release.

"You aren't crazy, Erin," Nick said. "You did see lions."

Lions?

Oh. She took a deep breath, willed her body to cool. Lions. Right. She had seen lions outside. She widened her eyes. "I knew it! Are they yours? Or do they belong to the owner of this place?"

"Well, yes and no. Lan and I own this place."

"Oh?"

Nick let out a harsh sigh. "Yeah, and the lions, well, they don't belong to us exactly..."

"They *are* us," Landon said.

Erin's jaw dropped open. "Huh?" How terribly, terribly sad. Her two lovers were completely insane. Time to escape...

"I want you to listen," Nick said. "Just listen, okay? Listen to what we need to say to you, and then we'll answer all your questions."

She nodded numbly. Fine, she'd listen. She couldn't speak right now if she'd had a gun pointed to her head. And they wouldn't harm her. Somehow she knew.

"We've been best friends all our lives. We belong to a pride of lion shifters," Nick said. "Our clan lives here in the Rockies. Landon and I grew up together. I was an orphan from another pride, and Landon's mother and father adopted me. Landon's father was our dominant male, but he passed on recently."

"Oh, I'm sorry." Sorry? She was sorry? That was what she

said after he'd just told her they were lion shifters? *Get a grip, Erin.*

"Thank you." Nick rubbed his stubbled jawline. "Anyway, I challenged Landon for the right to lead the pride as the new dominant male."

"You challenged your best friend?"

"Yeah. But it's acceptable. We're not fully human, Erin. We have some of our own rules."

Of course. How silly of her. "Go on."

"So we fought. Several times, actually. And no victor was declared."

"You would have fought...?" Nausea bubbled in Erin's tummy.

"To the death?" Nick's full lips curved slightly upward. "No. We're not like lions of the wild. What I mean is, we were so equally matched that neither of us could be defeated by the other."

"So"—Landon cleared his throat—"my grandmother, whose wisdom is honored among us, told us we were fated to both be the dominant males of the pride. It happens sometimes, when nature intervenes to add outside genetic material to what already exists. Our pride will be stronger with both of us as dominants."

"Uh-huh." Chills crawled over her. This was crazy.

Nick reached toward Erin and rubbed his calloused palm on her knee. "She's having a hard time, Lan."

"Of course she is. Wouldn't you?" He smiled. "My grandmother explained that when this occurs, the two doms share one mate, usually a human one, to configure even more genetic material into our mix. She said Nick and I would know her when we found her by her scent and by the ability to read her thoughts."

They *had* known exactly what she was thinking... Had answered questions before she asked them...

"It's you," Nick said. "You, Erin, are our mate."

"What?"

Landon took her hand, entwined their fingers. "You'll bear children to both of us. You'll strengthen our existence. And you'll be revered over all other females in the pride."

Right. Interesting. *Thud.*

★ ★ ★ ★

"Erin?"

Warm fingers stroked Erin's cheeks. She was on a bed. Her eyes opened and tried to focus. Two faces stared from above hers. Dark eyes, blue eyes.

Nick and Landon.

Sheesh, what a dream. "You guys aren't going to believe this."

"What?" Landon helped her ease upward. Nick held a glass of water to her lips.

She took a few sips. "I dreamed you guys told me you were lions and that you were the leaders of some pride of shifters and I was your mate." She giggled shakily. "Something else, huh?"

Landon smoothed strands of hair out of her eyes. "It wasn't a dream, baby."

She let out a sharp laugh. "Of course it was."

"We're going to have to show her," Nick said.

Landon nodded. "In a minute. Let her get her bearings."

Erin shot into a sitting position. "My bearings are just

fine, thank you. Show me what?"

"Don't be afraid, Erin," Nick said. "Remember how we made love to you last night? How much care we took? We would never hurt you."

"I'm not scared."

"We're going to shift for you," Landon said. "It's painful to shift, but it's also empowering. We enjoy it. So when we cry out, don't be alarmed."

"Huh?"

They stood, both naked and beautiful, and walked across the room, away from the bed.

"We need room," Nick said. "That's why our cabin is so big."

Erin's mind whirled. Lions? Completely impossible.

"Aaaauuugh!" Nick ground out. The pain sliced through the air in the room.

Erin watched, mesmerized, as golden brown hair sprouted from his skin and his body changed form.

Her heart ached. Oddly, she felt very little fear. Yet each snap of bone, each stretch of tendon rang in her ears and jolted through her body as if she herself were changing. But while she experienced the change, felt the wonder of it, the pain eluded her.

A beautiful animal was stealing Nick's shape. His jaw became more square, his head more round. As his nose morphed into a feline snout, sharp cuspids replaced human teeth. Hands and feet became padded paws, and the regal animal dropped to all fours. Lastly, his glorious mane sprouted like golden silk around his majestic head.

When the lion stood before her, his dark eyes smoldering, she stiffened.

"He won't hurt you, Erin," Landon said. "He's still Nick. He's still in his own mind."

Her emotions tumbled. Here came the fear. But also wonder. Her heart exploded with feeling, pure and awesome.

"My turn."

Landon cried out the same anguished moan. Again bones cracked, muscles shifted, hair grew, and again, the force of the change threaded through Erin. Landon shifted to the pale lion, almost white in the artificial light of the cabin. Searing blue eyes graced his leonine face. The tresses of his long mane swirled as he shook as a dog does after a bath.

They'd seemed catlike to her all night. The purring. The touching. Even the growling. Their beautiful slanted eyes. How they liked to rub against her.

But lions?

The evidence stood in front of her. She rose slowly, the backs of her knees pressing against the bed.

The darker one—Nick—advanced. A low growl rumbled across the thick nighttime air inside the cabin. She felt more than heard it.

Inside her mind a voice emerged. It's me. Nick. Don't be afraid. I won't harm you.

He walked slowly, the pads of his lion paws tapping softly on the plush carpeting.

He was so big! No wonder this cabin was huge. That mouth, those teeth—he could gobble her up in an instant.

Touch me, Erin.

Seemingly of their own volition, her fingers inched forward and buried themselves in the feathery golden mane. Warmth spread through her. The hair was coarse, yet soft, and it slid through her fingers like strands of linen thread.

Don't leave me out in the cold.

Landon's deep voiced hummed in her mind, and the pale lion crept forward with stealth. Soon she was caught between the two beasts, naked, their fur rubbing against her in slick vibrations. So warm. So amazing, the sensation of their giant animal bodies caressing her.

She closed her eyes, and their roars shook the room. When she opened her eyes, Nick and Landon, in human form, rubbed against her, one cupping her breasts, the other her ass cheeks.

"Will you, Erin?" Nick's voice was different. Deeper, more rumbly. Not quite human yet.

"Yes, love." Landon this time. "Will you?"

"Will I what?"

"Be with us," Nick said. "Mate with us."

"Oh, this can't be happening. I came here to"—she inhaled a deep breath—"to accept a new life. Life as a single woman. Not bound to anyone."

Nick plucked at her clit, and her legs wobbled. "That's not the life you were born for, honey. You came here to find us. You were led here."

"It's the truth, baby," Landon said. "We need you. You're ours, Erin. You belong to both of us. All of you—your body, your heart, your soul—is ours."

Her mind wasn't working. Thinking was out of the question. If she thought, she'd have to deal with the reality of the situation. And she would...eventually. Right now, though... right now, she wanted to feel. To bask in the bodies of these two beautiful men.

Men.

Cats.

Lions.

Human? "Are you...human?" she asked.

"Yes." Nick's fingers worked magic on her clit, snaked between the slick folds of her pussy. "Human. Human and feline. It's a rare gift."

"I never knew..."

"Most don't." Landon caressed her ass. "But we exist. Coexist. Peacefully."

"So will you, Erin?" Nick asked again. "We won't force you. But know this. You're ours. We won't find another."

"If I don't agree?"

"Then we won't mate," Landon said. "It's as simple as that."

"You won't...have sex again?"

Nick laughed. "We didn't say that. Felines are very sexual. Lan and I will definitely have sex. But we won't procreate. Only you will bear our children. Without you, our line will die out."

Ah. No pressure or anything.

Didn't matter. Her decision had been made. She wanted them. In some strange, inexplicable way, she *needed* them.

"You'll grow to love us, you know," Nick said. "It's in your blood. You may not believe it yet, but you will soon."

Love? She was halfway there already. Not just her body was involved here. She'd never imagined falling in love with two men. But now the idea seemed not only plausible but necessary to her existence.

She needed Nick and Landon, not only physically but emotionally.

Spiritually.

They were her destiny.

Yes, she said to them in her mind.

Their minds melded together. They understood. They were one.

From nowhere, an orgasm built within her, her pussy pulsed, her nipples strained, and rivers of boiling honey whooshed through her veins. A second later, she soared into the throes of climactic bliss.

We can do that for you. Their voices chorused through her soul. We can make you come with our minds.

Ah, heaven! Nick's lips came down on hers in a ferocious kiss. Landon's cock wedged between her ass cheeks.

Let us fuck you, baby. Landon.

Yes. Please fuck me.

Both of us. Nick. Both of us in your pussy at the same time. Just the three of us. Together.

Could they? Would it work? Though wet as a waterfall, she was only one woman. Only one pussy. A tight one, they had told her.

You will stretch and accommodate us. You were made for us.

Nick lifted her thigh, draped it over his sinewy forearm, and eased his cock into her wet cunt. Ah, fullness. But room existed for more. She could take two. Total satiety.

Nick backed her to the bed and lay down, Erin on top of him, presenting her already full pussy to her other lover. Landon's cock nudged her, and she reached behind her to spread her pussy lips and welcome him. His hardness nudged into her wet sheath.

One feminine body to take them both.

Hers.

Her mind whirled with emotion, vibrant images, incredible feeling. Jumbled thoughts. Words. Single words.

Then colors. Reds. Purples. And golds. Vibrant searing golds of a lion's mane.

Mate with me. Make me yours.

They obliged, fucking her hard. Fucking her fast. Her pussy expanded, took both of their cocks inside. Exquisite stretch. Sweet, slow burn.

Pure completion.

"God!" Landon thrust into her. "Your cock, Nick. It rubs against mine. It's..."

"I can feel every thrust," Nick said. "Yours and mine."

"She's ours, Nick. Our woman."

"Yours," Erin echoed.

Thousand of tingling arrows shot through her cunt, and the sensation built to fever pitch. Rainbows swirled through her mind, taking her higher, blazing, straight into the sun that rose outside the cabin.

Take me to the mountains, my lovers. My primal lovers.

Always.

She shattered, and her body splintered against the two strong men. As the walls of her vagina clenched both cocks, both men roared.

Two lovers.

Two amazing lovers.

"Is this really happening?" Her voice was husky, and her breath came in short puffs.

"It's happening," Nick whispered as he pulled his cock from her swollen pussy. "You know it as well as we do. In your heart."

"In your heart," Landon echoed, retrieving his own shaft.

Gently, they rolled her towards the middle of the bed, each snuggling against her.

"Time for sleep," Nick said.

Pianist Envy

CHAPTER ONE

As applause thundered around her, Jane stared at the chiseled face of the blond man who had been guzzling shots of tequila all evening. His full pink lips were pursed, his facial muscles taut. His fingers curled around his empty shot glass. While his companion cheered with the rest of the audience, he didn't lift a hand to clap. Clearly he was unimpressed with her and her music, but at least he hadn't gotten loud and raucous. Yet.

Jane eyed the red-haired woman sitting in the back. Lisa Taylor, agent extraordinaire, had come to this show just to see Jane Rock and the Stones. The set had gone well, and Jane smiled. Within an hour, God willing, her band would have representation and be on its way to the big-time.

"Encore, encore!" voices shouted.

Jane turned to Fernando, her bass player, and nodded.

"Thank you," she said into the microphone. "You've been a great audience." She signaled Lenny, her keyboardist, and began the count.

"Aw, fuck me! Not more of this musical atrocity!" The voice boomed above her count.

Jane turned to stare at that same man who held another shot glass to his shapely lips. His chiseled jawline tensed. She inhaled. *Should have followed your instinct, Jane, and asked to have him thrown out before it got to this.* He might look like a Greek god, but she was hoping the bouncer would have him booted.

"Hey, Jim!" she called to the large man sitting by the entrance. "Could you get rid of that guy?"

Jim, burly and balding, headed toward asshole's table.

Jane closed her eyes to clear her head. She tilted her head back and let her long dark hair tickle her bare back. *Feel the music, Jane. Let it take you.* The pure rawness of rock and roll always moved her. The cheers of the audience were icing on the cake.

She breathed in, visualizing success. Though regionally Jane Rock and the Stones had been headlining for a few years, they hadn't yet made it nationally. Lisa Taylor could change all that. Jane exhaled and opened her eyes.

"What the fuck do you think you're doing?" The asshole's voice was deep and just a little husky.

Sexy, actually—a bit of a contradiction to his clean-cut looks. Gorgeous, yes, but very clean cut, as though he had been reared on milk and corn with a side of caviar and educated at the finest prep schools in the country. His honey blond hair was cropped fairly short above his ears, and his striped cotton shirt screamed Ivy League. All he needed was tortoiseshell glasses to complete the look.

To cover those smoky green eyes, though, would be a sin. Even from the stage, they smoldered. Not Jane's type at all. No, she preferred long-haired rockers. Hmmm...asshole would look great with long hair. Wavy blond locks feathering around his perfectly-shaped face, dipping just a touch into those long-lashed green eyes...

"I'm kickin' you outta here, is what I'm doin'." Jim's Southern accent boomed over the din in the audience.

"I haven't done anything."

Jane grabbed her mic and took a deep breath. "You've

been rude all night," she said. "You've been drinking like a fish, and now you're interrupting my music."

Asshole scoffed. "You call that music?"

His companion touched his arm. "Calm down, Chandler."

Chandler. Perfect rich boy prep school name. "Uh, Chandler?" she said into the mic.

"What?" He jerked his arm away from his friend.

"If you have such a problem with my music, why exactly are you here? There are plenty of other clubs where you could harass the talent."

He scoffed again. "Talent?"

Jim yanked him out of his chair. "I said you need to leave, friend."

Jane's blood boiled. But she had the rest of her audience to think about. *Focus, Jane. Don't let him get to you.* She closed her eyes again. Time to get ready for her encore.

"I bet Jane Rock isn't even your real name!"

Her eyes popped open. Asshole, er, Chandler, again. Who did he think he was?

"Just something you made up to make yourself sound like a rock star."

Jane seethed and the hair on her arms stiffened. "Jim, please."

"I'm tryin', honey. The guy's stronger than he looks."

"I'm really sorry," Chandler's friend said. "He's had a rough week."

"Sure, whatever." Jane rolled her eyes upward.

When she looked back out into the audience, her stomach dropped. Jim lay flat on the floor with Chandler standing over him, a loafer-clad foot resting on the burly man's chest.

"What the hell?"

"He's a black belt in taekwondo," the friend said. "Shit, Chan, you're gonna get yourself arrested."

"Damn right you are." Jim's muffled voice rose from the ground.

"Fuck me," Jane muttered. "Ladies and gentlemen," she said into the mic, "I'm afraid we won't be able to offer an encore tonight after all. As you can see, we have—"

"Oh, please"—Chandler lifted his foot and Jim eased into a sitting position—"don't let me stop you. Continue with your noise."

That was it. "You think you can do better?" Jane's voice cracked, but determination won over nerves. "Come on up here and give it your best shot."

"With pleasure." Chandler stalked forward.

Jane tried not to stare. His green-and-white-striped button-down shirt covered his broad shoulders, and he had rolled his sleeves up, showcasing golden and muscular forearms. Crisp dark blue jeans covered what Jane instinctively knew were equally muscular legs. She readied to hand him her guitar, but instead he walked toward Lenny and the keyboard.

"Do you mind?" he said to Lenny.

Lenny raised his eyebrows at Jane.

She nodded. "Fine. Let's see what you've got. We're doing 'Come Back Alive.' There are several key changes, so try to keep up."

He sneered at her.

"One, two, uh, one two three!" Jane strummed her intro and the melody floated through her amplifier.

She'd written "Come Back Alive" when she was sixteen years old. She didn't usually play it in her sets anymore, but it was her classic encore song. She could play it in her sleep.

And indeed, she usually closed her eyes and let the music guide her as she sang. Today, though, she kept her eyes wide and focused on Chandler at the keyboard. She didn't want to miss his fuckup.

Fernando's bass joined in with low harmony, and Becca on the drums pounded a steady beat. Almost time for the keyboard. Lenny knew the song by heart, of course, and Jane didn't have to cue him. Damn if she'd cue Chandler, either. Let him figure it out on his own.

She jolted when he came in right on time. His smoky green eyes met hers as he matched every note, every chord, even adding intricate patterns to each melody and harmony that Jane had never heard before. This man made Lenny, an accomplished keyboardist, sound like a hack. After God knows how many shots, no less.

Jane jumped when Fernando nudged her. She looked toward him just as he mouthed the word "sing".

Sing! Shit, yes, she was supposed to be singing. She cleared her throat before she advanced toward the microphone and fell into the lyrics of "Come Back Alive." She closed her eyes, captured the colors and vibrations of the chords and harmony, swayed to the quickening beat.

Chandler's playing only made the music more beautiful, more evocative. She sang from her heart. Perspiration dripped from her hairline when she finished to booming applause. She took a deep bow and then turned to acknowledge Fernando, Becca, and finally Chandler. His friend in the audience whistled. Even Jim, who had recovered from Chandler's Karate chop, clapped, though less than enthusiastically.

Jane bowed once more and then looked past the audience to the entrance of the club. Two police officers stood silently, eyeing her new keyboardist.

Once the applause died down, Jane walked over to Chandler. His hands still hovered over the keys. And what hands they were! Large and golden, with long fingers that could work magic on Lenny's keyboard. What other type of magic might they work? How might they feel cupping her face, pinching her hard nipple, sliding in and out of her pussy or her ass?

Damn! She couldn't let his amazing looks mess with her head like that. Or his raw masculine fragrance—cloves mixed with fresh mountain air.

She shook her head to clear it. He sure as hell wasn't her physical type anyway, and even if he were, his attitude turned her off big-time.

She grinned at him. "That was a nice job."

He nodded. "I know music, unlike some people."

She resisted the urge to snipe back at him. "I can see you do," she said simply. "You're obviously well studied. But I'm afraid your time on this stage is over."

"Oh?" He arched his nutmeg eyebrows. "Maybe we should let the crowd decide who plays."

Jane cocked her head and tapped her boot softly on the stage floor, relishing what was to come. "First of all, the show's over. But even if it weren't, I think those cops over by the door might begin to lose patience. Unless I miss my guess, they're waiting for you."

★ ★ ★ ★

"What the hell were you thinking, Chan?"

The hammer in Chandler's brain pounded harder with

each of Ryan's harsh words. Damn, his head hurt. And the fucking sun was so bright! Had Ryan parked his car in the next county?

"Taking that bouncer down was just stupid. And giving that fine young thing on stage such a hard time. Look, I know you'd had a rough day, but was it worth getting arrested?"

Fine young thing? Hell, Jane Rock was beautiful, with a smokin' hot body that she showed off in her tight leather rocker outfits. Those long slender legs, those mesmerizing dark eyes, the onyx cascades of hair...and when she turned to face her drummer, her back had been bare and incredibly sexy. If only the strappy leather top had left her front bare too... He'd had a raging hard-on all last night watching her strut across that stage. Her voice was something else too—a natural alto with just a bit of rasp. Very sexy, even if she did use it to belt out discordant noise.

His groin tightened. But even thoughts of Miss Jane Rock's attributes couldn't dull the hammer. No, a jackhammer this time.

Ryan was still talking unusually loud and ridiculously fast, or so it seemed. Chandler had no idea what his friend was saying. Surely his brain would implode at any moment. "Christ, Ryan, I'll pay you back the bail money. Just shut the fuck up, okay?"

"I didn't have to pay any bail, moron, didn't they tell you?"

"Didn't they tell me what?" The last several hours had been a blur. Sharing a toilet with ten miscreants while nursing a drumming headache had never been on Chandler's "to do" list.

"The bouncer dropped the charges."

Chandler whipped his head around. Damn, that was a

mistake. The pounding increased. "He did?"

"Yeah, they should have told you."

"Hell, they might have. God, what is wrong with me?" He rubbed his temples.

"What's wrong with you is you drank too much. Just be thankful Jane Rock took pity on you when I told her your sob story and talked the bouncer into dropping the charges."

Chandler's neck tensed. "You told her?"

Ryan grinned. "Calm down. You know I wouldn't do that. I made something up. Said you'd been dumped by your girlfriend."

Chandler's muscles relaxed...a little. Humiliating, yes, but much better than the truth. The bouncer had dropped the charges. He should be thankful. Still, the thought of looking pathetic to Jane Rock rankled him, though he wasn't sure why. Who did she think she was, anyway, intervening on his behalf? He could damn well take care of himself.

He turned to Ryan. "Thanks, man. I owe you one for having my back last night."

"Well, I tried. I failed to keep you out of trouble, though."

"You couldn't have stopped me and we both know it. I was primed for trouble, and I think I found it."

"What do you mean?"

"A black-haired rocker named Jane. She won't get away with this."

"Get away with what? Getting your charges dropped?" Ryan shook his head. "You're something else, Chan. You ought to be thanking her." Ryan opened the door to his car and sat down in the driver's seat.

Chandler took his place in the passenger's seat.

"In fact"—Ryan started the engine—"you can thank her

this morning. I'm taking you to her place."

Chandler jumped in his seat and hit his head against the vinyl ceiling of the car. There went the jackhammer again. "You're what?"

"Did I stutter? I'm taking you to her place."

"Why in hell would you do that?"

"Because you were in no shape to drive last night, and neither she nor I wanted to leave your Benz at the club all night. The neighborhood's a little iffy, as you know."

Yeah, he knew. His Mercedes would have been stripped and sold for parts before sunrise. But why her? "Why didn't you drive my car?"

"Uh, I had my own car to drive. We met there, remember?"

Right. Fuzz still cluttered his mind. But again, why her? She was probably halfway to Mexico by now. In luxurious air-conditioned comfort.

Within a few minutes, Ryan pulled into a modest apartment complex on the outskirts of downtown. There it was—his luxury sedan—parked in front. At least it was covered under a carport. Had she used her own parking spot?

"Here you go, pal. She's in number 403."

Chandler widened his eyes. "You're leaving me here? You're not even coming up with me?"

Ryan let out a chuckle. "You're a big boy. You made your bed, now go lie in it." He shook his head. "I mean that figuratively, of course."

Ha! Chandler was in no shape to lie in anyone's bed at the moment, though Jane Rock and her perfectly sculpted body were certainly tempting. "You're serious."

"Totally. I have things to do today, and this isn't on the schedule. Get out."

"Some friend," Chandler muttered as he opened the car door and stepped onto the pavement.

CHAPTER TWO

Several hours in jail hadn't done anything to lessen Chandler Hamilton's physical appeal. The man was a god. Nature had certainly wasted a vast amount of beauty on the jerk. Even with his striped shirt wrinkled, his golden hair a mess, he was the most delicious hunk of flesh Jane had seen in some time.

"Hello, Chandler," Jane said as she held the door open.

"How do you know my name?"

"Ryan, of course, though I could have easily checked the registration in your yacht on wheels out there. You're Chandler Wade Hamilton the third, of blood bluer than the Pacific. I know all about you."

"Ah, yes. The curse of the family name."

"Ha! If it's a curse to have everything handed to you since day one, please"—she held up her hands—"let your curse fall upon me."

"Look"—Chandler raked his long fingers through his disheveled blond locks—"could I just have my keys?"

"Sure. Come in for a minute and I'll grab them for you."

He shuffled in slowly. Poor thing was no doubt exhausted.

Poor thing? Had that thought really just crossed her mind? The poor thing had heckled her all last night and had cost her Lisa Taylor's representation. By the time Jane and Ryan had talked Jim out of the charges, Lisa had already left, taking Jane's big break with her.

"Thanks for not wrecking my car."

She sighed. What an asshole! No use getting bent out of shape at his rudeness. "I do happen to possess a valid driver's license in the name of Jane Christine Rock. Which is my real name, by the way." She waved toward the couch. "Have a seat. I'll go get your keys." She hurried to her bedroom and retrieved them from her purse. "Here you are." She jingled them as she returned to the living room.

Shit. He'd fallen asleep on her couch. A soft snore sneaked from his throat. Just what she needed. She knelt down beside him and nudged him gently. Damn, his hard muscled shoulder felt wonderful beneath her fingertips. Better shoulders didn't exist on the planet, she was certain.

"Chandler, wake up."

"Mmmm." His deep voice rumbled, a husky caress.

Why the hell was this turning her on? Yeah, he may look like a god, but he was an asshole of major proportions.

"Damn it, Chandler, come on." She nudged him again.

"Mmmm. Jane."

"Yes, it's Jane. I'm right here."

One green eye slid open. "Mmmm. Beautiful Jane."

Beautiful? He gripped her forearm and pulled her downward until her lips were inches from his full pink mouth.

"Kiss me, Jane Rock."

Was he kidding? He raised his head slightly and brushed his soft lips against hers. Apparently not kidding. Electricity tingled through her and landed between her legs. Damn. From one little kiss?

Chandler's emerald eyes widened. Had he felt it too?

Within seconds Jane found herself on top of the tousled hunk, his hardness pressing into her thigh. His full mouth, lips slightly parted, beckoned. His breath was warm on her cheek.

Before she could think herself out of it, she pressed her mouth to his once more.

The tip of his tongue glided across the seam of her lips, and with each gentle caress, her skin ignited. Her breath caught and rasped out in a shallow pant when she parted her lips. He tasted of peppermint, and his tongue was sleek and warm against hers. She chased it, nibbled at it, sucked on its soft tip. Every cell in her body screamed at her to explore his mouth, to kiss him harder.

Yet she held back. This was Chandler Hamilton the third, asshole extraordinaire who had screwed up her chance with Lisa Taylor. She pulled away. "Look, Chandler, this is—"

His talented hands captured her face between them and pulled her back to his mouth. He thrust his tongue inside, not gently this time, but with a forceful domination that pulled her into his heat. Their lips slid against each other, and their tongues entwined and swirled together. Rumbling moans from his throat vibrated against the inside of her mouth and fueled her lust.

She wanted Chandler Hamilton the third. She wanted him to take her to bed.

After a few frenzied moments of kissing, he broke their connection with a loud smack and nibbled across her cheek to her earlobe. "Where's your bedroom?" he whispered.

Her mind a jumble, Jane slid off his hard body and grabbed his hand.

"Mmmm," his voice rasped from behind her. "Such a nice ass. Even in those gray sweatpants. But especially in that tight leather skirt you were wearing last night."

He had noticed? Through the haze of his drunkenness? She had sure noticed him despite his crass behavior. Even rumpled as he was, a finer specimen of manhood didn't exist at this particular moment.

Could she really do this? Sleep with him? She hadn't had sex in so long, he might find cobwebs down there.

She was dripping already, so wet she might not even feel him thrust into her. When she reached her bedroom, Chandler pressed her against the door, flattened his palms against the hard wood, and caged her. He pressed his erection into her lower back.

Oh, she had noticed while lying on top of him that nature hadn't cheated him in that department either. Didn't matter how wet she was—she would definitely feel his thrust. She inhaled a shallow breath.

"You're gorgeous." His raspy whisper caressed the sensitive skin of her neck.

Tiny ice drops penetrated the scorching blood in her veins. She shuddered.

"I want to slip inside you. Fuck you slow and sweet, and then hard and fast."

"God." She thunked her forehead against the door.

"I want to taste your pussy on my tongue, baby. I bet you're spicy. Then I want those ruby red lips around my cock." His soft mouth brushed against her neck. "I'll fuck you all day. All day long."

Jane slumped against the door. His words of seduction floated around her mind, jumbling and then unjumbling. She'd never gone to bed with a man she'd just met. Never slept with a man she didn't like. Nor had she ever gotten it on with such a fine hunk of manhood.

What am I doing?

His granite-hard erection thrust above the cheeks of her

ass. Oh, yeah. This was definitely going to happen. They were going to fuck.

The doorknob clicked as Chandler's closed his strong hand around it and turned. Jane nearly fell into the room, but he caught her and again his cock pushed into the small of her back.

"You have a tattoo here, don't you?" His breath feathered against the sensitive skin of her neck.

Tattoo? What was he talking about?

"Here." He pushed his arousal against her back once more.

Tingles shot through her. "What?"

"It's a dragon. I saw it on stage. Your skirt was cut so low, and your leather top showed your bare back. When you turned around to signal your bassist"—he let out a gush of air against the side of her face—"I saw the dragon."

"Oh?" Right, she had a dragon. Had been born in the year of the dragon. Thirty-fucking-four years old and still single. Still undiscovered.

And it was this man who had cost her the chance at discovery the previous night. What on earth was she thinking? She had to stop this. Yes, stop this...

His soft lips grazed the side of her neck and then her shoulder, as he pushed away the strap of her cotton tank. "I couldn't take my eyes off you." His breath caressed her upper arm. "I watched you the whole time I was on stage."

"But you..." Think, Jane. Get the words out. Forget how amazing his lips feel on you. "But you...never missed a chord. Never missed a note."

"Mmm." He rained tiny kisses along her shoulder blade and up the slope of her jawline. "I've had some training. Lots of practice."

"But to be able to follow so well, so elaborately..."

"Shh. I don't want to talk music right now. I want to worship your beautiful body."

"Oh, Lord..." Jane closed her eyes and let Chandler lead her to the bed. "I can't do this..."

He turned her to face him. His green eyes smoked. "Why not? You're here. I'm here."

Kisses. So many sweet sexy kisses. Tiny butterfly kisses to her chin, her throat. The sensual sting of his stubbled cheek rubbed against her.

"And I want you." He pushed his hardness against her flat tummy. "I'd bet my fortune that you're wet right now."

Uh, yeah. Dripping, to be exact. But that didn't change the fact that...

He slid one strong hand from her shoulder down her arm, to cup her mound. "Juicy, I bet. Spicy and wet and beautiful."

The friction of her sweatpants and undies against her clit prickled her skin. Her blood boiled.

"You want me," he said, his voice raspy. "You can't deny it, Jane Rock. You want me to take you to that bed and fuck you all day long."

God, she did! She wanted a good hard fucking. A pounding. Deep kissing, deep penetration. She wanted his cock everywhere—her mouth, her pussy, even her ass.

"Say it," he said. "Say you want me."

She opened her mouth to speak, but nothing emerged. Her body was on fire, engulfed in blazing flames. The blood in her veins had turned to boiling ambrosia and her skin was both heated and chilled. Sensory overload...

"Say it," he commanded again, his voice lower this time.

More sensual.

She closed her eyes, tipped her head back. His lips grazed the pulse point on her throat and a quiver raced through her.

"I want you. I want you to take me to bed."

He cupped her face and he thrust his tongue into her mouth. A deep kiss, a passionate kiss. Not a nice kiss. No, not nice at all. Possessive, primal, and very, very sexy.

A soft sigh escaped Jane's throat as she let her tongue tangle with his. Again his flavor, a mixture of peppermint and musky spice, assaulted her taste buds. She deepened the kiss, letting out soft moans that got lost in the passion of their mouths.

On the bed. How had they gotten on the bed? Jane lay flat on her back, Chandler on top of her, his jean-clad erection grinding onto her fleece-clad mound. So very good. Her skin prickled, her clit pulsed. She had never climaxed fully clothed before. Never...

He rocked against her, creating just the right rhythm, just the right beat.

"Jane." His voice was thick, husky. "God, Jane."

She moved with him, creating a complementary harmony to the melody of his motions, lifting her hips to bring their bodies closer, hating the barrier their clothes created.

Such immediacy, such fierceness mystified her, yet she couldn't stop. Oh, no. Didn't want to stop.

Again she moved upward, crushing her clit against the hardness in his jeans. Such a subtle movement, only a graze really, but she burst into flames as the pulsing climax rolled through her. Starting in her pussy, it radiated into her legs, her belly, upward to her arms and to her cheeks. Why did she always feel a great orgasm in her cheeks? She had no idea, but she did. Tiny tingles needled over her face and she knew her color had turned a rosy pink.

"Oh!" Her voice came from above her, or so it seemed. She continued to grind up against Chandler and the contractions kept coming, each bringing her more and more sensation.

"Oh, damn, baby. Damn. You're so hot." He brushed his lips against her warm cheek. "Do you always come this easily?"

No. Never actually. But she wasn't about to tell him that. "Depends."

"On what?"

On whether I haven't had sex in ages. On whether the man I'm with knows instinctively how to touch me, rub against me... "Just depends. You know."

He let out a gruff chuckle. "No, I don't know, but right now I want in your pants so bad I don't care. You can explain later." He rolled off her and began to undress her. With haste. First her sneakers and socks, and then her sweatpants and cotton panties. "Wow." He inhaled, closed his eyes. "I can smell you. So ripe, baby."

Ripe? Hell yeah. She was ready to fall off the vine. Even more so now that she'd experienced an orgasm executed by this gorgeous man. She wanted more. Lots more.

He opened his eyes and regarded her moist pussy. He inhaled again. "Not only fragrant but beautiful too, just like I knew you would be." He inched her legs farther apart. "So pink, baby. So pretty."

Pretty? No one had called her pretty down there. Sure, men had appreciated that part of her, sometimes only that part of her, but no one had taken the time to really see it like Chandler did now.

He moved, seemingly in slow motion, and licked his full

red lips. "I'm going to taste you, Jane Rock."

God, please! She didn't need to say the words aloud.

His tongue stroked her wet slit, silky smooth caresses. Her pussy still pulsated minutely, must still be open and pink for him. The thought turned her on. Jane closed her eyes and turned her cheek into her pillow. She loved having her pussy licked, and right now her clit was on overload from the climax. When he kissed it she would—

"Oh!" The slurpy kiss to her swollen nub sent sizzles straight to her core.

"Mmm, good baby?"

More than good. She was at a loss for words. A simple groan escaped her throat.

"You taste amazing. Just like I knew you would." He tugged on her swollen pussy lips, shoved his tongue inside her channel.

She writhed beneath his expert ministrations. A god on the keyboard and a god in bed. Who could ask for more?

"Turn over, baby." His mouth grazed her inner thigh. "I want to see that dragon. I want to lick you from behind." Gentle hands guided her as she moved onto her tummy. "God you've got a nice ass." His breath tickled her butt cheeks. "But I've already told you that."

Oh, yes, he had.

"Beautiful work." He lightly traced the outline of her tattoo.

"Thank you."

"I've always wanted a tattoo."

"You don't have one?"

"My mother would have a cow."

Jane jolted and craned her neck to face him. "Your

mother? Are you serious? How old are you, Chandler?"

"Twenty-nine." He smiled. "Born in the year of the cock."

She couldn't help but laugh. "Seems appropriate. But I guess you don't want to tattoo a rooster on your back. Or a giant dick." She paused. "Still, you seem older. I'd have guessed we were around the same age."

"Stuffy prep schools and expensive conservatories make a man seem older, but"—he gave her ass a sharp swat—"I assure you I'm old enough to make you feel absolutely amazing. Now where were we?"

He slid his silky tongue between the cheeks of her ass and toyed with her puckered hole. She shivered. She wasn't a huge fan of ass play, but right now it made her whole body tingle. After a few moments of wet caresses, he stabbed his tongue inside her.

"Chandler..."

"Hmmm?" His voice vibrated between her cheeks.

"I don't think—"

"Shh. Don't think, baby. Just feel."

Good point. She closed her eyes and nestled into her pillow. He probed her ass with his tonue, and a moment later, a further breach.

"Just a finger, baby. Don't be afraid."

She wasn't. She breathed deeply and willed her tight muscles to stretch. Chandler's touch was penetrating. And strangely erotic.

"Have you ever been fucked here, Janie?"

Janie? "Uh...no. No I haven't."

"Well, you think about how this feels. My finger sliding in and out of you. And you decide if you want to feel something else down here."

Oh, she wanted it. She had no idea why, but she wanted nothing more right now than for Chandler to shove his dick in her tight little ass. So she felt more than a whimper of loss when he withdrew his finger from her snug hole.

"Do you know what?" Chandler said.

"What?"

"We've been having all this fun and I haven't even seen your breasts yet."

"Ha! I haven't seen your anything yet." Jane turned and sat up. "I'd say I've gotten the shorter end of the stick so far."

A smug grin touched his full lips. "Trust me, baby, you won't get a short stick."

Before she could think of a comeback, he crushed his mouth onto hers and lifted her tank top. He deftly unsnapped her bra and discarded both it and the top. He cupped her breasts and thumbed her hard nipples.

Electricity shot to her pussy. She had long believed that her nipples were somehow connected to her pussy. Very sensitive, and she loved having them pinched, licked, sucked.

"Very pretty, Janie. Beautiful. Great nipples."

She sighed. "Thank you."

"I love the color. Dark. Almost a brownish purple. Gorgeous against your light skin."

Color? She'd never had any man mention the color of her nipples before. Clearly, though, Chandler Wade Hamilton the third was not just any man. She jerked backward when his lips brushed a nipple.

His forehead wrinkled. "You okay?"

"Yeah, yeah. Of course. Fine. It just...feels good, that's all."

He chuckled. "Well it's supposed to feel good. Sure feels good to my lips." He bent down and continued.

Melodic sensations slid over Jane, gave her shivers, culminated in her pussy where her clit throbbed. He'd already made her climax once, had begun to show her the pleasures of her ass, and now was treating her breasts to gourmet licking and tugging. And he hadn't shed one piece of clothing yet.

"Chandler..."

"Hmmm?"

"What...what is going on here?"

"We're going to fuck, baby."

"Yeah..." Sounded great, but... "We can't do this."

"Why not?" He nibbled at her areola.

Keep your head, Jane. "Because. We don't...know each other. We don't like each other..."

"I like you fine right now." He let her nipple drop with a soft pop. "But maybe you're saying you don't like me?"

"Well, you..." She closed her eyes. Couldn't look at that handsome face and those lips swollen from kissing her. That body that had rocked her out of orbit. "You don't like my music."

"What the hell?" He scooted away from her, but remained on the bed.

She resisted the urge to lean back into his warmth. "You heckled me all last night. Got yourself arrested because of it. And now you're here, wanting to fuck me?"

He scoffed. "Yeah. Don't know what I was thinking." He stood, still clothed. "I should have my head examined." He rubbed his temples. "It's still pretty fuzzy up there. You are beautiful, but definitely not my type."

Jane's heart sank. She had hoped... Well, she had hoped they would continue despite her own misgivings. She'd hoped he'd be persuasive, show her how much he wanted her. Instead, he obviously had his own misgivings. She should be thankful he'd come to his senses. Not filled with a sense of loss.

"Maybe we could—" The phone rang, interrupting her thoughts. "Sorry. Excuse me for a minute."

She grabbed her cell off the nightstand. Becca. "Hey there."

"Jane," Becca said. "I have great news and not so great news."

Jane's tummy did a flip-flop. Well, not so great was better than terrible. And great was...well...great. "Give me the great."

"Lenny went to see Lisa Taylor at her hotel and begged for a second chance. She's coming back to Rodney's tomorrow night to hear us. He fixed it with the owner and everything to have us play on a weeknight. We won't get paid, but he figured it was worth it."

Jane's feet actually left the ground. A jump for joy. "You're kidding? What was he thinking? But who cares, it worked! That's so great! But why isn't *he* calling?"

"Well, sweetie, that's the not so great news."

There went the tummy flop again. "Shit. What is it?"

"On the way out of the hotel, a cat ran by him." Becca's sigh hissed through the phone.

"So a cat ran by. So what?"

Becca cleared her throat. "Well, a big dog was chasing the cat, and he knocked Lenny down on the sidewalk." A pause. "He broke his wrist."

Jane's breath caught. "Geez. Is he okay?"

"He's fine. He's at home resting. Fernando and I are on the way over to his place to see him now."

"Thank God." Then it sank in before Becca said the words.

"But we play for Lisa Taylor tomorrow night, and we're shy one keyboardist."

CHAPTER THREE

Thank God she had stopped him. What had he been thinking? About to sleep with a woman whose music he despised.

Well, not despised exactly. More disrespected. Even that wasn't quite the right word, but her rock and roll represented everything that was wrong in his life, the bane of his existence.

And the biggest problem? He had enjoyed himself last night. He had felt the music, felt the rhythm. He had felt Jane. The woman had talent. Major talent and an incredible voice. She was going places. While he...

Well, at the moment, Chandler was going nowhere.

"Not sneaking out on me, are you?" Jane's husky alto flowed by him as he touched the door to her apartment.

She sang even when she talked—amazing. He turned. She was beautiful. She'd put her rumpled sweatpants back on. Plus her tank with no bra. Those sexy tits hung lusciously inside the gray cotton. Nipples protruding. God, were those her dark areolas peeking through what was supposed to be opaque fabric? They had felt so wonderful against his lips, his tongue. Tasted so smooth, so delicious. Fucking imagination!

He cleared his throat. "I figured we were done here."

"Chandler, Chandler, Chandler." Her tone was mocking, even a bit caustic. She approached him, her derriere swaying temptingly. "We're so not even close to done."

Oh? Had she changed her mind? Because he could easily change his. Inferior music aside, the woman was smokin' hot.

He stroked the soft skin of her inner arm. "If you say so, baby."

She jerked her arm away. "Uh...not going there again, Mr. Hamilton."

Ouch! Major rejection. Too bad his boner didn't react. It still throbbed in his jeans. He steeled himself against her loveliness. "Then what do you want?"

"It seems I have a little problem."

"I'm sorry to hear that." He rubbed his thumping temples. When had his headache returned? "I'll leave you to deal with it as you see fit." He reached for the door.

Her warm hand clamped onto his forearm. Damn, her touch set him on fire!

"I'm afraid it's not that simple."

"I'm sure it is, if you'll excuse me—"

"Chandler, you owe me."

Huh? "For what? Taking care of my car? I'd think the privilege of driving such a fine piece of machinery would be payment enough, but if you need a few bucks, I—"

Her hand shot out quicker than he could react. The sting of her slap warmed his unshaved cheek. There went the jackhammer again.

"I do not need or want any money from you, you ungrateful asshole!" Her cheeks reddened and her nostrils flared.

His face ached, but still his cock stood stiff inside his jeans. Even angry she was the hottest thing walking.

She let out a sigh. "But I do need you, and you owe me."

"If you don't want to sleep with me, I can't begin to think what you'd need me for."

She clenched her small hands into fists. "You infuriate me, you know that?"

"The feeling's a bit mutual, baby. What is it that you want?

I'm aging here, and my head is about to explode." And so was his dick.

"Take some ibuprofen then," she said, "and I'll brew you some fresh coffee, because you're playing keyboard for me tomorrow."

Had he heard her right? He jerked his neck around to follow her as she walked toward her kitchenette. *Yes, she has a great ass, Chandler. Stop gawking.* "What the hell are you talking about?"

She fiddled with a canister of coffee, scooped out several spoonfuls into a paper filter. "It's simple, actually. Last night an agent came to see the band. Because of your little indulgence, she left before we got a chance to talk. My keyboardist, Lenny, went to her hotel this morning and convinced her to come back tomorrow night."

"Great. Good for him. Now goodbye, Jane Rock."

"I'm not finished yet." She poured water into the coffee maker. "Lenny's had a little mishap. Broken wrist. That leaves us short one keyboardist."

Fuck. He knew where this was going.

"Since you blew our chance with the agent last night, and clearly you're an accomplished keyboardist—"

"Pianist." He shuddered. "I'm a virtuoso pianist. Not a keyboardist."

"Potato, po-tah-to," she said with a smirk. "You know your way around a keyboard, you're here, and you owe me."

"If you think I'm going to tarnish my reputation by playing in a rock band—"

"You didn't mind tarnishing your reputation last night."

"In case you didn't notice, I was a little inebriated last night." As his pounding head continued to remind him.

"There's something you should know about Lenny," Jane said.

"Yeah? What's that?"

"Well, he's not a virtuoso pianist like you are, obviously. He's self-taught, on his grandmother's old upright. He plays by ear. Pretty amazing, really, considering he dropped out of school in eleventh grade to help his mother pay the bills. This break was as much for Lenny as it was for me. For Becca and Fernando too. None of us has had it easy, Chandler. We've worked hard to get where we are. We deserve better, and you're going to make sure we get it."

"Look, I'm sorry about Lanny—"

"Lenny."

He sighed, massaging his aching temple. "Whatever. I'm sure he's a great guy, but I can't play with your band. It's not my kind of music."

"You did just fine last night, as you know." The muscles in Jane's beautiful face tensed. "Must be tough, huh? To have everything you ever wanted handed to you? The best schools, the best instruments? I bet you play on a Steinway at home, don't you?"

He did, but he wasn't going to admit that to her. So his family had money. Why did people constantly want him to apologize for that?

"I've always wondered where I might be today if I'd had an education like that." Her voice softened, and her eyes glazed over. "At least I was able to finish high school. But like Lenny, I'm self-taught. My aunt gave me a used guitar for my tenth birthday. I picked out chords on my own. When I couldn't figure anything else out, I bought instruction books at a secondhand music store and taught myself." She looked intently at him, her brown eyes slightly sunken.

What was he supposed to say to that? Again, he refused to apologize for his good fortune. Besides, his money couldn't buy everything. Disappointment still existed for Chandler Hamilton the third. A fact that had been drummed into his brain recently.

She didn't wait for an answer. "I envy you. I really do. I wish I had had your opportunities. Who knows where I'd be today? Platinum albums, maybe a Grammy or two. I could buy my mom a house, a car..." Her eyes misted.

God, please don't cry. He didn't think he could take that.

"Well, my problems aren't yours." She wiped the edge of one eye with her finger and took a solid stance as she flipped the switch on the coffee maker to "on." "Except for this one. You're my keyboardist tomorrow night. And you're not going to let me down."

He closed his eyes. He had to. The misty torment in her dark smoky eyes haunted him. Then there was his dick...hard as steel, pulsing against jeans that seemed tighter by the second. His arms longed to hold her, his hands to caress her skin soft as suede, his cock to breach her tight passage and make love to her.

He could give her the comfort she craved, the comfort he craved as well. God, he wanted to, wanted to embrace her, kiss away those tears that seemed likely to fall at any moment, make her forget all the hell that had put that forlorn look on her beautiful face.

He inhaled and opened his eyes. Had he ever seen a lovelier woman? Not in this lifetime. Without responding to her or waiting for the coffee she'd promised, he walked silently to the door and left.

★ ★ ★ ★

Thank God she and Ryan had exchanged cell phone numbers. The next day, Jane stood outside Chandler's private piano studio, address provided by Ryan. She'd spent a sleepless night worrying about Lenny, not to mention the audition for Lisa Taylor, which was mere hours away now. The few times she drifted off to sleep, she'd awakened in a sweat, images of Chandler Hamilton haunting her. He'd left so abruptly the day before and she hadn't had the chance to get his contact information.

His friend Ryan was nice, much nicer than Chandler. "He'll most likely be at his studio practicing," he'd said.

"He has his own studio?" she'd asked, before realizing what a stupid question it was. Of course he had his own studio. He was Chandler Hamilton the third.

Nothing about the small studio screamed out the Hamilton name, however. It was a modest little building in a secluded part of town bordering on rural. She'd tried calling Chandler first, number also provided by Ryan, but he hadn't answered. She'd left a voicemail, but couldn't rely on him to call back. So here she stood outside the little studio. She breathed in and knocked on the door.

No response.

If he was rehearsing, he no doubt wouldn't hear the knock anyway. Boldly she turned the knob. To her surprise, and to her relief, the door opened. She entered a small reception area. No one sat at the mahogany desk or on the adjacent sofa and chairs. A coffee pot and paper cups sat on a little table next to the desk. Brown liquid filled the pot, but there was no brisk aroma of fresh brew. She touched the glass. Cold.

"For God's sake, this is ridiculous," she said aloud. Did he never empty the pot? It would grow mold for sure. She picked up the pot and wandered down the small hallway to the right of the reception area. Restroom. That would work. She entered and poured the rancid coffee into the sink, rinsed out the pot, and pushed open the doorway.

She readied to walk back to the reception area when a chord of notes trickled to her ears. They were soft yet angry, as though they were being pounded through a wool blanket. Of course! A wooden door stood next to the restroom. Chandler's studio would be soundproof. The fact that the notes met her ears proved he was playing very loud.

She didn't bother knocking. He wouldn't hear her anyway. Normally she wasn't so rude, but the music called to her. His anger, his passion, called to her. Still holding the pot, she stood, mouth agape, as Chandler pounded out disharmonic chords on his nine-foot black lacquer grand.

Disharmonic, yes, but they made a certain musical sense. Discordant in a harmonic way.

Sweat covered his brow, and a drop hit an ivory key. He didn't stop to wipe away the perspiration. He punished the keys, ground out eerie yet beautiful music in his raw madness. His fingers danced, his facial muscles tensed, his full pink lips pursed.

Another drop of sweat hit a key as he slowed the tempo, softened his strokes, and then from *piano* to *forte* again as he trilled two notes and boomed through the lower keys.

Jane's heart thudded in time with Chandler's now increasing tempo. As he crescendoed, so did she, her breath coming in rapid puffs, her breasts heaving against her chest. His playing conjured images in her mind of a bullfighter twirling a red cape. Vivid reds and oranges swirled through her head.

More chords. Louder, faster...banging, clashing...

Then silence.

His eyes closed and his chest dropped, as though he were only now cognizant of the fact that he required breath. More drips of moisture emerged on his corded neck and rivered down his chest through the few blond hairs that peeked out of his black button down. The stark onyx contrasted against his fair skin in a beautiful way.

Jane's breath caught. She stood, still holding the empty coffee pot. Should she applaud?

Her hands were occupied, and applause seemed inappropriate anyway. This hadn't been a performance. No, this had been a catharsis, a purging of negativity, a ritual cleansing. This had been solely about Chandler. Pure, raw emotion not meant for an audience.

Regret flooded her. She shouldn't be here.

She turned as quietly as she could, hoping to sneak out before he became aware of her presence. Her hand hovered above the doorknob.

"Don't tell me." Chandler's voice.

She turned.

"Ryan, right?"

She sighed. "Yes. I didn't know how to reach you about tonight."

He didn't reply, simply closed his eyes and inhaled a visible deep breath.

"I'm sorry I interrupted you." Jane cleared her throat. "But it was brilliant. Truly. You're incredible."

His eyes popped open. "It's an elementary composition. I played it in concert when I was eleven."

Jane shook her head. Couldn't the man take a compliment? "Well, I've never heard it before. Of course I'm not educated in the classics as you are. I thought it was amazing. What is it?"

"Danza del Fuego."

"Sorry, I don't speak Italian."

He smiled. Actually smiled! Those gorgeous lips parted to reveal perfect white teeth. "It's Spanish, not Italian. It translates to Ritual Fire Dance. It was written in 1915 by Manuel de Falla."

"I've never heard of him." She inched forward slightly, drawn in by his smile, which hadn't yet faded. "But I should have known it was Spanish. It reminded me of a bullfight. I kept imagining reds and oranges."

"That would be the fire." His smile broadened. "It's from a ballet called *El Amor Brujo*, Love the Magician. In this piece, a girl is haunted by her dead husband's ghost, so she performs the fire dance. The ghost appears and dances with her and is drawn into the fire. Then she's free of him."

A purging. A ritual cleansing. Oh, yes, she'd been on the right track. Chandler was trying to let go of something.

Well, of course he was. Ryan had said he'd just been dumped. He must have really loved her.

An anvil hit Jane in the stomach. She had been nothing more than a salve to ease his heartache yesterday. He hadn't wanted her. He'd just wanted to get laid. Anyone would have sufficed.

She let out a breath she hadn't realized she'd been holding. What did she care, anyway? He obviously detested her music. He probably detested her, as well. She was nothing more than a warm body.

She shrugged her shoulders in an attempt to dislodge the

yearning invading her. Despite the fact that his smile made her blaze inside, he was nothing more than a warm body to her as well. But he was a warm body who could play the keyboard for her tonight.

She cleared her throat again. "I'm really sorry I interrupted. I just stopped by to finalize the plans for tonight."

"Tonight?"

She let out a huff. "Yes, tonight. You're playing keyboard for my band, remember?"

He smirked. Damn him, he was still gorgeous when he smirked!

"I don't recall agreeing to that."

"I don't recall giving you choice. You owe me, remember?"

He stood and rolled his clear green eyes upward. "Baby, if there's one thing I'm certain of, it's that I don't owe you, or anyone like you, a goddamn thing."

Jane's skin prickled as anger surged through her. "You're not letting me down, damn it. Play for me tonight, I get an agent, and I'm out of your hair forever."

He inched toward her. She trembled, nearly dropping the glass coffee pot.

"What if I don't want you out of my hair, Jane Rock? What if I want to fuck your brains out right on top of my Steinway?"

She widened her eyes. Her heart riveted. "What?"

"You heard me."

Oh she'd heard him all right. Though she longed to fling herself into his muscular arms, words emerged on her lips. "Are you crazy? That Steinway must have cost a hundred grand!"

His lips curved into a lopsided grin. "Closer to two hundred, but it's a little plain, don't you think? Could use some ornamentation. Your naked body would look rather nice draped over it."

Flutters raced through her tummy and settled between her legs. Why did he do this? Act like he hated her one minute and then come on to her the next? And why didn't she possess more strength against his charms? Which really weren't charms at all. He wasn't a nice man. "I..."

"At a loss for words, Janie?" He inched forward again, slowly, until only a foot separated him. Heat radiated from him.

Or was it from her own body? "No...it's just..." She shook her head to clear it. "You know I need a keyboardist tonight—"

"Pianist."

"Yes, pianist. Whatever. Fuck." She sighed. Maybe it was better not to keep telling him he owed her, even though he did. That seemed to piss him off. "I don't just need a keyboardist. Or a pianist. I need you, Chandler. The audience loved you. You're amazing. Please?"

He closed the gap between them, took the empty coffee pot from her hands, and set it on the floor. "Maybe we can make a deal."

"What do you want?"

His eyes blazed. "I thought I already made that clear. I want to fuck you on my Steinway."

Red heat scorched through her. Was she angry? Or turned-on? Both, it seemed. "I'm not a whore," she said, willing her voice not to crack. "I won't barter my sexual favors for your time tonight."

His grin broadened. "Don't think of it as any kind of payment. It's more like you scratch my back and I scratch yours. It'll be an enjoyable little interlude for both of us. And you will enjoy it, trust me."

Of that she had no doubt. He was clearly a master of seduction. She'd learned that yesterday.

"The fact is, I want you," he continued. "I don't want to want you, but I do. I haven't stopped thinking about you." One long finger slowly trailed up her forearm. "You're not my type at all0"—he shook his head—"but damned if I can get you out of my head."

His soft touch in the crease of her elbow made her shudder. Just a graze, yet wetness dripped into her panties. "So if I...sleep with you—"

He let out a harsh sigh. "I hate euphemisms, baby. This isn't sleeping together. This isn't making love. This is a fuck, pure and simple. You're hot. I want to fuck you."

How did he do that? Make her feel desired and wanted one minute, and then like a common slut the next? She didn't have much, but she did have her pride. She swallowed. "Sorry. Thank you for the compliment—I think—but I'm not interested in a fuck right now." Though her wet pussy begged to differ. "I'm interested in a keyboardist—sorry, pianist—for my band tonight. But I'm not willing to sell my body for it."

Chandler closed his eyes and took in a deep breath. "God. That only makes me want you more. You're killing me." He opened his eyes and pierced her with their smoky jade beauty. "Fine. I'll play for you whether you fuck me or not. But I hope you'll fuck me. I want you so badly. You have the sweetest cunt I've ever tasted, you know that?"

Cunt. Had she ever heard the word spoken aloud? Not in this lifetime. But it was dirty, nasty. And God she liked it.

"You get so wet, so juicy," he continued. "And your asshole is so cute and pink and tight. Fuck." He shook his head. "If I can't have you at least once I think I'll go insane." He gripped her shoulders.

His touch singed her. If not for his grip she'd be a mass of jelly on the floor, she was sure of it.

"Are you attracted to me at all, Janie?"

Had he really just asked that question? She'd nearly fallen into bed with him twenty-four hours earlier. She opened her mouth, but no words emerged.

"I think you are." He stroked her cheek. "I think you want me as much as I want you. That's what you said before. You responded to me yesterday. You got so fucking wet for me."

"I..." She couldn't think. His hand on her face was so hot, and yet so gentle.

Who was he? Was he the arrogant ass who wanted a quick fuck from a hot woman? Or was he the heartbroken man who made her feel wanted and desired?

"I want your juices pooling on the lid of my piano." His already deep voice lowered. "I want to pin you down, shove my hard cock in your sweet little pussy. Tell me you want that too, Janie. Tell me, and I'll give you the best fuck of your life."

Rational thought fled her brain. She wanted him. How could she deny it? He was gorgeous, talented, and he ate pussy like a champion. "Yes, Chandler, I want you."

He crushed his lips down on hers in a frenzy of raw passion. The kiss was hard, even painful at times as his teeth gnashed against hers. Their tongues dueled, their lips meshed, muffled grunts escaped both their throats. Chandler paused, drew a ragged breath against her lips, and set about devouring her again. Was it possible he deepened the pressure of his strong mouth? Yes, he did. More passion, more primal need flowed from him to her, and she returned it with equal ardor.

Her arms crept upward and she grasped his sculpted

shoulders, warm beneath the black cotton of his shirt. Animal instinct took over. She trailed her fingers to his collar and ripped the shirt open. Buttons hit the hardwood floor with several small pings.

The curve of his lips smashed against hers. He was smiling. She could feel it. One strong arm moved downward and a hand plunged inside the waistband of her jeans.

He broke the kiss and trailed his moist lips to her ear. "Are you wet for me, baby?"

She whimpered as he sifted through her curls and reached her sodden core.

"God yes"—his voice was husky—"so wet for me."

She pulled his shirt out from the waistband of his jeans and pushed the fabric off his shoulders. He freed one arm, but the shirt hung on the other as he continued to rub the lips of her wet pussy.

"Too many clothes," she said against his golden neck. She kissed him, nibbled him.

His chuckle rumbled against her cheek. "We can take care of that. But I have to stop touching you."

Stop touching her? She might die! "No. Touch me. Put your finger in my pussy. Please."

"Oh, baby, I'll be happy to. But let's get naked first and I can do it so much better."

Yes, naked. That's what she was after. She forced her lips from his flesh and moved backward, dislodging his hand from her inside her pants. Quickly she started to pull her T-shirt over her head.

"No. Let me." Chandler reached beneath her shirt and caressed her bare belly. "I want to unwrap you."

"But that'll take too long."

He let out a short laugh. "Yes, I can see you're in a hurry." He brushed the remaining sleeve of his shirt off his arm. It fell to the floor in a heap. "But I want to savor you, Janie. Let me undress you." He fingers stroked her skin as he pulled the shirt off her slowly.

"This is madness," she said, her voice breathy.

"Well, we're a little mad, aren't we?" He pulled the shirt over her head, tossed it to the floor, leaned down, and buried his face in her cleavage and kissed the tops of her breasts. "Isn't that what a good fuck is? What passion is? A little bit of madness?"

Yes. He made perfect sense. "Like the piece you were playing."

When he nodded, strands of golden hair tickled her.

"That piece is pure madness. But it's not what I'm feeling now. Right now I'm mad for you. Mad with passion, not anger or regret. If I can't have you, I'll go even madder with lust." He growled against her throat as his deft fingers unhooked her bra and discarded it.

Her ample breasts fell gently against her chest.

"You're fucking beautiful. They're perfect." His lips closed around one hard nipple.

She groaned as his touch set her afire. *Danza del Fuego*. Ritual Fire Dance. The chords rang her in head as he tugged on her tight bud and then licked it. First bite, and then soothe, and each sensation traveled at light speed straight to her clit.

Ah, yes, there existed more than one meaning to the cleansing fire dance. Chandler was getting over a woman. And Jane? Well, she hadn't had sex in a long time. This was pure fantasy for her. A pure dance of fire and passion. Perfect.

He moved to the other nipple and kissed it, worshiped

it, as he continued to knead the first between his thumb and forefinger. "Gorgeous breasts, Janie," he rasped against her areola. "Perfect."

She sighed. She couldn't stand much longer. Surely she would melt soon.

As though he'd read her mind, her nudged her backward, toward the piano, until her bottom hit the smooth wood. Good, at least it was something to lean against. He bent and took her mouth again in a possessive kiss. His bare chest felt like heaven against her breasts, and his hard cock nudged against her bellybutton through the barrier of his jeans.

Why hadn't he gotten naked yet? She tried to say as much, but her words were muffled by his kisses. He rained tiny pecks on her cheeks, her eyelids, her forehead.

When he reached her ear, he whispered, "I can't get enough of you. Your scent, your touch. You drive me crazy!"

Crazy. Mad. Those same words again. They described her feelings as well. "Take off your pants, Chandler," she said boldly. "I want to touch your cock."

"Oh baby," he rasped against her neck, "I will, and you won't be disappointed. But good things come to those who wait. First I'm going to rid you of the rest of your clothes, set you on top of that piano, and eat your juicy pussy till I'm ready to burst."

Moisture gushed from her. Her panties were already saturated. Now her jeans themselves were no doubt wet. Chandler worked at the snap and then the zipper. He fell to the ground and tugged off her sandals. Soon her jeans joined his shirt and hers on the floor.

He lifted her—what strong arms!—and carried her to the piano's shiny keyboard. With a discordant plunk, he set her onto the keys. Their coldness shocked her, but only for a millisecond. Her body heated through.

Chandler pulled up the black bench and sat, his giant erection apparent beneath his jeans. He stared at her pussy—simply stared—until Jane was sure she would burst open.

"So pretty, Janie." He traced her outer lips with one finger. "And so wet for me."

The slight caress of his finger nearly sent her over the edge. She closed her eyes, inhaled. "For God's sake, Chandler, eat me!"

"Oh, I will, baby. Can't I admire the artwork first?"

"You're driving me crazy!"

He chuckled. "Seems to be the theme of the day. Craziness. Madness. Right now I'm insane looking at this gem between your legs. You're so beautifully made. You remind me of a cute little Mozart sonata."

A soft giggle erupted from her throat. "Is that supposed to be a compliment?"

He nodded. "The highest compliment. Mozart made the most complicated music sound so simple. When I look at you, I see how such a simple thing as a pussy, something all women possess, can be the most beautiful thing in the world when it's attached to a woman I desire so strongly. Your lips are full and meaty, your cunt wet and pink, your clit swollen and wanting. So hot, so inviting." He looked up at her and smiled. "And don't even get me started on that cute little asshole of yours." He traced a path from labia lips down her perineum to rub her tight opening, moist from the pussy juice that had trickled downward.

Jane's heart stomped, nearly out of her chest. His mouth had descended and he was tonguing her ass. Probing it. God, it felt good.

"But my pussy, Chandler. I want your mouth on my pussy!"

His head bobbed up. "You don't like what I'm doing?"

"Fuck. I love it! But if you don't eat my pussy I'm going to die right here!"

His smile warmed her. "We can't have that." He slid his tongue over her clit.

She shattered. The orgasm hit her full force, seemingly from nowhere, much like it had the previous day. Was this man some kind of sex god? How could he make her come so easily?

"Fuck, baby, you're coming aren't you?"

Jane couldn't answer. Her body quivered in time with the contractions in her pussy. Discordant notes banged out as her palms came down on the ivory keys.

"I love how you come so quickly for me, so hard for me. Let it take you. Enjoy it. There're plenty more ahead."

Jane's skin tingled, her heart skittered. She closed her eyes, opened them, closed them again. When the climax finally ceased, she opened them and met Chandler's hot gaze.

"I couldn't take my eyes off you," he said, his voice cracking. "You're beautiful when you come."

Her pussy gushed nectar again. And then again.

CHAPTER FOUR

Chandler couldn't stop staring at her beautiful pussy. Had she understood when he'd compared it to a Mozart sonata? He wasn't sure he understood himself. He'd had plenty of pussy in his life, but Jane's hypnotized him. Its color was unlike any he'd ever seen, a deep plum, almost like the skin surrounding her delicious nipples, but a softer hue, like a new burgundy. A Beaujolais Nouveau even. Her firm lips dangled below the opening begging to be sucked. The inside was a luscious pink that mirrored a dry rosé. Why he was thinking about wine at a time like this baffled him. But never before had he compared a woman's genitals to a piece of music either.

Jane Rock was something else. Beautiful seemed such an inadequate word to describe her. Dazzling. Yes, that was better. His Jane dazzled.

His Jane? *Get a grip, Chandler. This is a fuck, nothing more.* He could still worship that amazing pussy, though. Would she taste as sweet as she had yesterday? He couldn't wait any longer to find out. He looked up at her pretty face, so serene and lovely with her lids heavy, her cheeks flushed from her climax. Her dark hair was in disarray. The next time he kissed her he'd sink his fist into those silky tresses and pull her to him by the hair. So hot.

For now, though, he had a gorgeous cunt to eat. And God was he starving! He snaked his tongue between her silky fold for the tiniest taste. Mmm, still so sweet. Her lips were sleek and soft against his tongue. He'd never felt such a satiny texture. Her cream dampened his mouth with honeyed sweetness. Rich and thick, it floated on his tongue. Pure essence of Jane.

A soft sigh left her lips. "Yes."

"Mmm. You like that, baby?"

"Yes, yes. I love it."

"I could eat you all day. You taste so good, Janie." He delved into her tight passage, tasting the inside of her. Tanginess mingled with the sweetness on his tongue. So perfect, so tantalizing.

Another sigh. She made him crazy!

"I want to taste your ass again."

She lifted her thighs, held them back for him, and exposed herself.

What was it about her? First he was waxing poetic about her pussy, and now her ass. He'd never been this enamored with a woman's asshole before. He tongued her sweet little opening, listened to another soft sigh.

"Your finger, Chandler. I want your finger."

He continued to lick her ass as he breached her tight pussy with first one finger, and then two. Her suction—and more of her sweet sighs—welcomed him as he drilled her.

"Yes, just like that." She let her legs drop and forced him to release her ass.

It saddened him to let the puckered hole go, but he had plans for it later. For now he twirled his tongue around her clit as he finger-fucked her. When her channel started to clamp down, he knew her orgasm was coming. No, he wanted her to come while he was inside her. He released her clit and removed his fingers.

"Chandler?"

"I love how you come for me, Jane."

"I didn't come that time," she huffed.

He let a broad grin spread across his face. "I know."

She pouted. "You sadist."

"Baby, I promise you you're going to come as many times as you want to, but the next time you do, my cock is going to be shoved all the way inside your delicious little cunt."

"Well, Mr. Hamilton, there's a problem as I see it."

He widened his eyes, let his smile fade. "What might that be?"

Her eyes gleamed. "How do you expect to get your cock inside me when you still have your freaking pants on?"

His shaft throbbed against their denim barrier. "You do make an excellent point." He pushed the piano bench away. It skidded across the hardwood floor, and in a flash his shoes, socks, jeans, and boxers mingled with the other discarded garments. "Shit." He picked his jeans off the floor and rustled in his pocket for his wallet. When he found the condom, he ripped it open quickly and sheathed himself.

"Chandler!" Jane sat up. Piano notes, high and low, clashed.

Had he done something wrong?

"What?"

"You put a rubber on!" she whined.

"Of course I did. Safe sex and all. Don't you want safe sex?"

"Yes, I want safe sex! But I didn't get to suck your cock! I didn't even get to look at it, touch it..."

God, as much as he wanted her sexy mouth on his hard dick, he was ready to go for the gold right now. "Later, baby, I promise. Right now I have to fuck you." He thrust into her tight passage.

Home. Not so much the word but the concept permeated his mind as her warm flesh engulfed him. The dulcet moan that left her lips floated to his ears like the sweetest melody.

"Jane, you're so tight." He winced, trying desperately to hold on, not come too quickly.

Tiny spasms started at the base of his cock, and his skin froze. He held himself taut, immobile, deeply embedded in her moist channel until they subsided. How could she hold him so snugly? So securely? As though she were created for him?

When he'd regained his composure, he reached beneath her bottom, clinking rattled chords as he cupped the firm cheeks of her ass and tilted her hips upward. Rotating his pelvis, he began a slow rhythm removed from the frenzy he was feeling. A descant to the raucous melody of voices in his head urging him to fuck her hard, fuck her fast.

"Chandler," Jane's alto rasped, "do you have another condom?"

He circled his hips slowly, grinding into her. "Yes. Why?"

"Thank God!" She jumped off the keyboard, dislodging his cock from her pussy.

He wasn't sure he'd survive the loss.

In an instant she was on her knees before him, peeling the condom from his erection. "Because I have to suck your cock!"

"Fuck," he growled. Her soft lips felt almost as good as her pussy. He closed his eyes, and then opened them. He'd much rather watch. "Suck it, baby. Just like that."

She swirled her tongue around the head of his cock, licked his pre-cum. He'd been close to coming before, but this was ridiculous. The urge to grab her head and fuck her mouth like he wanted to fuck her pussy overwhelmed him. That long beautiful hair beckoned. He stroked the locks, testing the waters a bit. Her moan fueled his lust, and he gripped each side of her head.

"That's it. Let me fuck your sweet mouth." He pumped into her, letting her take all of him.

Was that the back of her throat he nudged? He felt, more than heard, the husky moan that vibrated against his cock head.

"You like to suck cock, baby?"

Her head bobbed.

"Yeah? You're great at it." She was.

Damn, he wanted to come. He wanted to force every last drop of cum down her throat, watch her swallow, watch her take all of him. But he had to come in that hot pussy. Had to.

"Baby."

Her gaze shot upward, her eyes locked with his.

"I need to fuck your pussy now. I want to come inside that hot little body of yours."

She whimpered, but let his dick dangle from her full lips. "You didn't like that?"

"Are you kidding? I loved it. I wanted to come."

"You could have."

"Fuck, you're amazing! And I hope to spill in your mouth sometime. But what I really want right at this moment is to fill that beautiful pussy of yours."

She dropped her gaze to his hardness. Had he gotten bigger? Sure felt like it.

"That's one beautiful cock, Chandler."

His skin warmed. He was well-endowed, no doubt. But words of praise for his manhood had never meant more to him. He didn't stop to ponder why, just fumbled around for his jeans, grabbed another condom, and was inside her wetness before sixty seconds had passed.

"Janie, you hold me so snug." He pumped. He thrust. Her tight passage welcomed him. Icy sparks skipped over his skin. "I can't hold on, baby. I have to come. Are you close?"

Her breath puffed against his neck covered in sweat. "Just touch my clit, Chandler. Touch it, and I'll come for you."

He removed one hand from her narrow hip and sifted through her nest of curls to find her swollen nub.

"Yes," she breathed, "like that. So good."

As soon as her contractions started, his balls tightened and his own tiny spasms started at the base of his cock and surged forward. Lightning coursed through his body as he spurted his semen into her warm and welcoming cunt.

"Jane!" he yelled, his voice nearly unrecognizable. "Jane, I...I..." One last thrust brought the last stream of cum from his tip embedded deep inside her.

His whole body tightened, shivers rushed through him, nothing existed except him and the dazzling woman who took him within her wonderful body. He collapsed against her warmth as the violent shudders slowed and then ceased altogether. "Wow."

"Wow yourself, Chandler Hamilton. That was amazing." She stood, and notes chimed as her firm ass slid over the keys. She began gathering her clothes, which were strewn about the floor.

What a travesty to cover that amazing body.

"So," she said, zipping her jeans, "I need you there at six o'clock tonight for warm up. We play at nine."

Chandler didn't answer. Real life smacked him in the head with a vengeance. Their fuck had been exactly what he'd told her it would be. A fuck. Nothing more. So why had he expected it to mean more to her? Certainly it had meant nothing to him other than sinking his dick in the prettiest pussy he'd ever seen. He'd gotten his rocks off. Exactly what he'd wanted.

"Chandler?" Jane pulled her shirt over her head, covering her beautiful breasts. Her bra still lay on the floor. "Did you hear me?"

He didn't meet her gaze. Instead he picked his own clothes off the floor and donned his boxers and jeans.

"Chandler?"

He thrust his arms into the sleeves of his black cotton shirt. Fuck. No buttons. Jane had ripped them off.

"Chandler?" Now she was in his face. "So you're just going to ignore me now?"

Uh, yeah. That had been the plan. But he could no sooner ignore Jane Rock than he could ignore his own cock, which was coming to life just because she stood in the same room as he. "What is it, Jane?"

"I said I need you at the club at six tonight."

He rolled his eyes skyward. "Six. Whatever."

Her flushed cheeks reddened further. Her dark eyes smoldered, but not with lust this time, with the fire of anger. "You can't let me down."

"I never made any promises to you."

"You did!" She balled her hands into fists. Her whole body tensed. God she was beautiful. "You said if I slept with you—"

"And you said you wouldn't whore yourself out to pay for my time. This was a fuck, baby. A simple fuck. We both got what we wanted. There was no deal other than that."

"There was! You said you'd play for me whether I fucked you or not."

Shit. He *had* said that. Funny what lust does to the brain.

"Damn it! You owe me!"

Owe her? Why did it burn him up when she said that? He shook his head. He knew exactly why. "I think I've made it clear that I don't owe you, or anyone like you, anything."

"Why do you keep saying that? What do you mean by anyone like me?" She shook her head, let out a huff of air. "Look, I know your girlfriend just dumped you, but that doesn't mean you can—"

Now his own hands balled into fists. Girlfriend! If only it were that simple. "You don't know anything about me, Jane. All you know is that I enjoy fucking you. That's the culmination of your knowledge about me. So don't presume to understand what I'm going through."

"Christ, we've all been dumped, Chandler."

He fiddled with a button hole. "You owe me a shirt."

"I'll buy you a dozen shirts, okay? I'll hand sew new buttons for you. Just don't let me down tonight. Please." Her eyes misted.

Now she was offering to buy him shirts. Hell, the shirt he wore had probably cost more than what she made in a week, and she was offering shirts. He felt like a piece of shit.

A yearning to take her into his arms overwhelmed him. He wanted to hold her, kiss her, ensure her he'd always be there for her, starting with her performance tonight. That he'd never let her down. Ever. Instead he walked out the door, his shirt hanging open and untucked, and left her standing alone in his studio.

★ ★ ★ ★

"You can't let her down, Chan."

Was that his conscience speaking? No. He looked up from the bench in the backyard of his family's mansion. Ryan stood there. Of course. It had been his conscience. Ryan had always filled that role.

"Since when are you Jane Rock's champion?"

"She's a nice girl. You ought to spend some time with her, get to know her a little."

Get to know her? He knew her. He knew her in the biblical sense. It didn't change anything. "So you know her, Ryan?" A stab of jealousy pierced his gut. "Just exactly how do you know her?"

"She and I talked pretty extensively the night you were arrested, and we talked on the phone earlier today. She was looking for you. She's a smart woman with a lot of talent."

Chandler closed his eyes, inhaled. "And she's beautiful."

"Oh God..."

Chandler met his friend's gaze. "What?"

"You slept with her, didn't you?"

"What makes you think that?"

"You've got that starry-eyed 'Chandler's in love' look. Christ, I haven't seen that since Katie Dorman your first year at the conservatory."

Chandler looked away. "I don't know what you're talking about. Jane Rock is nothing but a thorn in my side."

"Ha! A thorn in your side, maybe. A thorn in your heart? For sure." Ryan fumbled with the keys hanging from his side pocket. "Look, she deserves this break."

"Yeah? Where's my break?"

Ryan shook his head. "You're something, you know that? You're whole fricking life has been one big break. Jesus, Chandler."

Shit. Ryan never called him Chandler. Always Chan or buddy. Still, there were some things even his best friend didn't comprehend.

"All my money couldn't buy me my dream."

"Money never can. You know that."

Chandler sighed. This wasn't news to him. He knew his money couldn't get him where he wanted to go, and he hadn't depended on it. He had worked his ass off, but to no avail. "Ryan, you know I've never expected to buy my way anywhere."

Ryan sat down next to him. "Yeah, I know that. You're a good guy, Chan. You always have been. But right now you're being a little shortsighted and you know it."

Yes, he knew it.

"Jane didn't cause what's bothering you."

"But—"

"It doesn't matter. It wasn't her. You're a rational person. You're letting this one failure blind you. Do something nice for someone else. It is, after all, your fault that the agent didn't stick around the other night."

"Thanks for the salt in that wound."

"What do you expect from me? Lies? I wouldn't be a friend if I let you get away with this self-indulgent crap. You fucked up, and Jane paid the price. Now you can fix it for her. This isn't a hard decision. It's not a decision at all. It's something you have to do."

"I don't have to do anything!"

Ryan stood and raked his fingers through his dark tousled hair. "True enough. I've had my say. I can only hope you come to your senses. You're not a selfish person. You never have been. I'm proof of that. So don't let one event color your life."

Chandler said nothing.

"If you don't come to your senses, I swear I'll come and drag you by the hair if I have to. You're not going to let her down, Chandler. Especially if you feel something for her. Grab the brass ring, bud. Don't let her go." He walked away.

Chandler buried his face in his hands. Envy. Jane had said she envied him. Why shouldn't she? He'd had it all—the money, the education—but where had it gotten him? Here. It had gotten him here. Sitting on a wooden bench feeling sorry for himself.

Truth be told, he envied Jane. Her break was coming. He was sure of it. Lisa Taylor would sign Jane Rock and the Stones. She'd be a fool not to. Jane not only had the voice of an angel, she had charisma, she had intelligence, she had drive. Not to mention a rockin' body and the most incredible pussy he'd ever had the pleasure to taste.

She had it all, including him. Fuck, yes. Him. He wanted to see her again, but she'd never agree. He'd made sure of that.

Damn it! He had nothing.

He wiped his brow, rubbed his eyes. For the first time in his life, he had no idea what to do.

CHAPTER FIVE

He'd better not let me down!

Jane glanced at her watch. Chandler hadn't made any promises. He could easily not show. He'd already missed warm up. Lenny had offered to do what he could one-handed. She'd take him up on it if she had to.

Damn you, Chandler!

"Hi, Jane."

Not Chandler's voice, but familiar. Jane turned to see Ryan standing in the door of her small dressing room. She hadn't realized she'd left it open. "Ryan. Where is he?"

"He's coming. I swear I'll see that he doesn't let you down."

"Do you know where he is?"

"I can always find him. I'll personally deliver him to you if he doesn't show up. But have some faith, Jane. He's not a bad guy. He'll do the right thing."

Not a bad guy? Jane's feelings for and about Chandler boggled her own mind. She was wildly attracted to him. He made her skin heat, her pussy pulse. She got wet just looking at him, and making love to him—correction, fucking him, he'd been very clear about that—had taken her places she'd never been.

And his talent! *Danza del Fuego* still thrummed in her head, in her heart. An elementary composition, he had said. She couldn't wait to hear him play something difficult!

"I hope you're right," she said to Ryan. "I need him

tonight."

"There's still time."

"He missed warm up."

"I'm sorry about that. I'll find him for you if it comes to that."

She smiled. "Thanks. You're a friend. What do you see in him, anyway?"

Ryan chuckled. "We've known each other a long time. Grew up together actually."

"Really? So you're blue blood too?"

Ryan grinned. He had a crooked smile, lips not as full as Chandler's, but very attractive nonetheless. His rugged dark looks contrasted nicely with his friend's wholesome corn-fed appearance. Faded jeans and an AC/DC T-shirt. Chandler would never wear that. Never in a million years, despite the fact that he'd look amazing. Ryan also looked amazing in a totally different way. Very sexy.

"I'm afraid my blood's as red as yours. My mother was the Hamiltons' maid. I lived in their house."

Jane widened her eyes. Wow. Not what she'd expected at all. "And you're close?"

"Best of buds almost our whole lives. Even when he went away to school we kept in touch. And the Hamiltons put me through college. State university, not a private conservatory like Chandler, but they didn't have to do it."

"No, they didn't." Lucky Ryan. What she would give to go to college! "So his family's nice?"

"They're great. Very generous."

"Okay." Confusion tensed her forehead. "Why is he such an asshole then?"

"He's not, Jane. He's had...a rough couple days."

"Yeah, I imagine it's rough having everything handed to you. Great education, all the money in the world. Not to mention killer looks and a perfect body."

Ryan let out a chuckle. "He works for his body. He eats right and works out."

"And drinks like a fish."

"Like I said, that's not really him."

"Right. He's had a difficult few days. You can see I'm playing my violin over here."

Ryan smiled weakly. "It's not an excuse for what he did to you. You're absolutely right."

Jane let out a sigh. "Look. I know his life is far from perfect. Money can't buy happiness and all that." She shook her head. "I just wish I'd had all the opportunities he's had, you know? It's tiring sometimes, knowing I have the talent to make it but never having had any formal instruction. If I'd had his education, I wouldn't be wasting it getting drunk and calling out other musicians."

"It's not him."

"So you've said." She adjusted her black lace top.

Too much cleavage? Probably, but part of her act was how she looked. She wasn't just selling her music. She was selling an image. Just one more thing she envied about Chandler Hamilton. He didn't have to market an image. He had the education to back up his talent. He could make it on his musical ability alone.

But here stood Ryan, a product of Chandler's family's generosity. Could there truly be a part of Chandler she wasn't seeing? He had been gentle in her bedroom and again in his studio—well, not exactly gentle, but she wasn't complaining. He certainly hadn't pressured her or forced her into anything she didn't want to do. She smiled.

"Chandler's right."

Ryan's voice startled her. For a moment she'd forgotten he stood there. She licked her lips.

"Right about what?"

"You're beautiful."

A jolt of happiness surged through her. "He told you that?"

"Yeah. This afternoon when we talked. He's been through some major shit."

"Right, his girlfriend. We've all been there, Ryan. Getting dumped sucks, but it's no reason to turn rabid."

Ryan visibly tensed. His lips pursed.

"You okay?"

"Yeah. I'm fine. There's a story there, but it's not my story to tell, Jane. I'm sorry." Ryan edged toward the door. "He'll be here. I promise you."

She turned toward her mirror to check her makeup.

"What are you doing here, Ry? Moving in on my territory?"

The image in the mirror startled Jane. Chandler's familiar body moved behind Ryan's. He wore a crisp forest T-shirt and black jeans. Trying to look the part? She wasn't sure, but he looked scrumptious. Absolutely fucking edible. Thank God. He was here. He'd play well, she was sure of it.

"Just convincing Jane that you wouldn't let her down," Ryan said. "And see? I was right."

Jane turned to face both men. Such a contrast. One blond and refined, one dark and rugged. Both gorgeous in their own way. Had they ever shared a woman?

She shook her head to clear it. Where had that thought come from? And what had Chandler meant when he'd said "my territory"? Did he have feelings for her? She intended to find out.

"Your territory? I beg your pardon?"

"For tonight, I mean." Chandler cleared his throat, and his cheeks reddened. "Your band is my territory."

Jane smiled. Right. And she had some swamp land in Florida to sell. He liked her. He'd made that clear this afternoon. But something more was brewing in her own mind, her own heart, despite his contradictory words and actions where she was concerned. Was something more happening with him? Could they get past the fact that he hated her music? There was one way to find out for sure.

She stepped toward Ryan, wrapped her arms around his neck, and kissed his lips. She didn't expect what happened next.

Chandler closed the door and moved behind Jane, brushed his lips against her neck. "You ever had two men, baby?" he whispered huskily in her ear, his breath a soft caress against her neck.

She broke the kiss, and Ryan's lips traveled over her cheek to her ear. He licked her lobe. Tugged on it. Her muscles tightened, and electricity sizzled beneath her skin. She'd just been wondering if he and Ryan had shared women. How could they be so in sync?

Energy whirled around her. Her body was hypersensitive, hyper-aware. Every nerve on alert. She was burning alive from the inside out. Burning with passion.

"Have you, baby?" Chandler asked again, nuzzling her other ear. "Two men?"

"N-No," she stammered, her voice not quite her own. "N-Never."

"Have you thought about me?"

The vibrations of his deep voice scorched her soul.

"Have you thought about this afternoon?"

Truly, she'd thought of little else. And had berated herself repeatedly for thinking it. But now wasn't the time or place. "You have to warm up. The set... Lisa Taylor..."

"We have an hour and a half before we go on, princess." He trailed tiny kisses over her bare shoulder. "I'm warmed up, trust me. Getting hotter all the time. And I'd like to show you how two men can pleasure a woman."

"But you...you don't even like me. You don't..."

"I like you just fine. And so does Ry."

"I think you're beautiful," Ryan agreed. "I'd love the chance to pleasure you. Just this once."

Just this once? What did that mean? Incoherent thoughts and images swirled inside her head. Moisture pooled in her pussy. But her costume, her makeup...

Hell, she was in her dressing room. She could fix everything quickly if need be. And she already knew Chandler would be brilliant whether he warmed up or not. He'd proved that the last time.

When would she have the chance for a threesome again? The fifth of never, no doubt. She'd most likely never see either of them again after tonight.

A pang of regret flooded her heart. She didn't want this to be the end. She wanted to see Chandler again and again.

But why let sadness reign? That was her last thought. She resigned herself to only feeling. Letting the music—for it *was* music—take her to a new height of awareness. The melody of Chandler's lips on her neck, the sweet caress, the soft cadence. And the harmony of Ryan's tongue on her earlobe, the underlying beat. As if he knew his place—an important part of the equation, but this was Chandler's song.

Chandler moved his hands down her arms, and they clasped hands for a moment before he reached under her lacy spandex tank and traveled slowly up her tummy to cup her breasts. He coaxed, caressed, tugged at her hard nipples. Jane moaned and moved her hips in circles, grinding into Chandler's hardness behind her.

From the front, Ryan pressed his arousal against her belly. She grabbed his shoulders and molded his hard body to hers. Two men pressed against her. Two men pleasuring her. Ryan lifted her tank over her head and bent his head to kiss one of the breasts that Chandler held out in offering.

Jane sighed, leaned her head back onto Chandler's shoulder as he kissed her neck and fondled her full breasts. "You've done this before," she said.

"We have." Chandler nibbled the outer edge of her ear. "Does that bother you?"

A little. But only about Chandler, which was odd. Why should she care how many women he'd been with? How many women he and Ryan had pleasured together?

Because she was falling for him, that was why. It hit her like a thunderstorm. What she'd felt brewing in her heart.

She didn't answer Chandler. Just sighed again and let the music take her. Chandler let go of Jane's breasts and let them fall gently against her chest. Ryan took over, cupping and squeezing them as he licked and tugged a nipple. His lips were softer than Chandler's and his touch more gentle. He squeezed her other tight bud, again his stroke lighter but no less stimulating.

Jane's pulse raced. Her pussy contracted, and her clit

throbbed. Emotion, thick and heady, surged through her. Raw need to be taken by these two men consumed her. Chandler's tongue traced patterns on her lower back. Her dragon. He was licking her dragon.

"Very sexy, Lady Jane," he said. "So very sexy." He eased her miniskirt over her hips until it puddled at her feet. "Mmm. Sexy thong." He removed it. "Sexier without it."

"Oh God." Her voice was a soft sigh.

He was tonguing her asshole again. Pleasure coiled within her. Ryan's fingers left her nipple, trailed to her clit, and massaged it gently with her juices.

Intensity. Liquid heat. She could easily lose herself forever right here in her dressing room. End up as moisture on the floor. At the exact moment Chandler breached her tight hole, Ryan entered her slick pussy with a finger.

She erupted like a volcano. The climax took her outside of herself, high above the clouds. She heard herself speak, but could make no sense of the language. Fire and ice raced through her as her muscles relaxed, her pleasure ascended.

"That's it, let it take you," Chandler said. "Come for me, baby."

Yes, for him. Though Ryan was there, was pleasuring her, this climax that coursed through her was for Chandler. Somehow she sensed that all three of them understood.

As she came down from her high, Ryan's steely cock pressed against her belly. When had he taken off his pants?

"You ready, baby?" Chandler asked as he eased his finger from her tight hole. "Ready for me to fuck you?"

She whimpered, nodding.

"On your knees, beautiful. I'm going to take you from behind while you blow Ryan. Sound good?"

Better than good. Amazing. Again she whimpered as she fell to her knees. The cheap carpet in her dressing room scratched her skin, but she didn't care. All she cared about was having Chandler. Having both of them. Having Chandler.

Ryan's cock head nudged her lips. He was big, nearly as big as Chandler, and his cock was a lovely golden color.

"Go ahead. Suck him. It'll turn me on."

Jane winced a little. She had been waiting for Chandler's permission. How had he known? She hadn't even known until he said it. Slowly she tongued the tip of Ryan's cock. Mmm. Salty and delicious. She loved giving head. Loved being able to bring a man to his knees with bliss. Couldn't wait to suck Chandler's cock again.

Right now, though, Ryan deserved her full attention. He was sweet, handsome, a wonderful man in his own right, and she wanted to suck his cock, wanted to give him pleasure. Ryan grabbed her ears as she nibbled and licked, first the underside and then his balls as she inhaled their musky scent. She slid her tongue up the length of his shaft and swirled it around his swollen cock head, letting the tip of it nudge inside his tiny slit. His rumbling moans fueled her passion and she sucked harder.

"Oh yeah, that's it, baby," Chandler said from behind her. He gave her ass a sharp swat. "Take all of him. Show me how much you like to suck his hard cock."

Warmth from Chandler's hand soothed the sting from his slap. Sparks skittered across Jane's flesh, and her pussy throbbed in time with the plunges of her mouth onto Ryan's thick cock. The rip of a packet reached her ears. Condom. That meant fucking. Chandler was going to fuck her now.

God, she couldn't wait to feel that giant erection in her pussy again. She sucked Ryan deeper, letting his tip graze the back of her throat.

He groaned. "Fuck, she gives good head, Chan."

"Yes she does. You like sucking cock, don't you, Jane?"

She nodded. Couldn't speak. Wanted to speak. Wanted to yell at him to shove that hard cock in her pussy. Right now!

"Ah!" She moaned, her mouth full of cock, as Chandler thrust into her.

She grabbed at Ryan's hips, dug her fingernails into his flesh, and continued to blow him as Chandler sank into her more deeply. Filled her. Filled her as she had never been filled before.

He was large, oh, yes. But he filled another part of her as well, even more than he had this afternoon. Something deeper and more powerful. He reached inside her soul and shared her music.

"Damn you feel good," Chandler said. "So fucking tight. You're amazing, baby." He slammed into her again. "So amazing."

"I'm going to come," Ryan said. "I can't hold off any longer."

"Not unless she says it's okay." Chandler thrust again, even harder and deeper this time. "Can Ry come in your mouth, baby?"

She nodded. She didn't mind. She loved it, actually. Had yearned for Chandler's semen on her tongue earlier. Couldn't wait for that pleasure...

"Ah, God!" Ryan erupted, and his cum coated her tongue.

Salty, a little bitter. She swallowed, licking the last remnants from his cock head. Still Chandler pumped into her.

Ryan's cock fell from her lips, and he knelt and kissed her, a soft brush of a kiss, only a little tongue, only a little passion.

This was a kiss of friendship.

"Thank you, Jane," he whispered against her chin.

She smiled. No man had ever thanked her before. Chandler's thrusts slowed, and she pressed her lips to Ryan's cheek. "Thank you too," she said, "for everything."

Ryan sat back as Chandler caressed her hips.

"Turn around now, baby," Chandler said. "I want to kiss you while we fuck." He rolled her onto her back and mounted her.

Plain old missionary had its advantages, like deep kissing with a lot of tongue. The passionate kissing she and Chandler were sharing now. Their lips meshed, their tongues tangled, their groans mingled in each other's mouths. Where was Ryan? She couldn't bring herself to care at the moment.

Chandler was her world. All that existed. He pushed his thickness into her, matched each thrust with his tongue in her mouth. He tasted of peppermint again. Peppermint and horny male and soul-searing passion. He possessed her, filled her, and she clung to him, let him sink further and further into her body, into her heart.

The peak rose in the distance, and she climbed again, stood on the precipice. One more thrust...and she flew, the climax even stronger this time. Strong enough to pull out a piece of her soul. She cried out as she came down, lifted her hips so he could take her further.

"God, baby, I love how easily you come for me. I felt that in my toes. Every pulse of your pussy. I need to come. Come in you."

A desire surged deep within her. She wanted to taste him. Wanted his semen on her tongue more than she wanted her next breath. "My mouth, Chandler." Her voice came in rapid pants. "Come in my mouth."

"Aw, fuck. Yeah, baby. God, yes." He withdrew and climbed over her, his cock slick with her juices and poised against her lips.

She opened for him, let him take her, let him control as he fucked her mouth while she lay still on the floor. He tasted tangy—a mixture of their two flavors. He pumped steadily, never going far enough to choke her.

"Baby, I have to come."

She nodded, hoping he understood that she wanted him to come. Wanted to give this to him. Wanted his cream on her tongue, in her body. He shot into her mouth and she savored it—let the zesty sweetness coat her tongue.

When he withdrew his penis, he slid down her body and covered her lips with his. They kissed, sharing his taste, sharing their passion. His heart beat against her chest, a rapid cadence that matched her own. As the kiss turned from frantic to gentle, he rolled to the side and pulled her body against his. She ran her fingers over the damp skin of his shoulder as he nibbled at her lower lip. She closed her eyes, and sweet emotion enveloped her.

CHAPTER SIX

"Where did Ryan go?"

Chandler kissed the side of her neck. More thrills shot through her.

"He knows when to make his exit."

"Oh."

"We share women from time to time. To give the woman something special. But when it's a woman he wants, I make an exit when I can. And vice versa."

Her heart skittered.

"Are you saying you want me?"

He laughed. "I'd think that's pretty obvious at this point."

Jane sat up. Checked her watch. Forty-five minutes until show time. "We need to get ready. I wish I had a clue what you were talking about, but we don't have time right now to figure it out."

He grabbed her hand. "We have a few minutes. I need to tell you something."

"That you hate my music?" She scoffed. "I already know that. You like my body, hate my music. Well, Chandler, I am my music."

He sighed. "I don't hate your music. For God's sake, I happen to think you're incredible."

"You do?"

"You mean all of our amazing sex hasn't convinced you of that?"

She couldn't help but smile. "It was pretty amazing."

"You're so talented, Jane. You're going places. I know it. You've said you envy me. To be truthful, I envy you."

"Me?" Jane whipped her head around to look into his smoky green eyes. For a moment she thought she could see into his soul. He spoke the truth.

"It was my idea to go see you play the other night."

"You're kidding."

"Nope. Ask Ry. He'll tell you. I'd heard you were something special, and I wanted to check you out."

"But you don't like my music."

"It's not that. I do like your music. Am I a huge rock fan? No, I'm not. I'm a classically trained pianist. But I recognize talent. You've got it. And frankly, you're headed in a direction I'm not. It's hard for me."

She frowned. "What do you mean? You're wonderful. You made that keyboard come alive last night."

"I didn't expect you to be as good as you are." He feathered a finger over the sensitive skin of her inner arm. "And I certainly didn't expect to come alive when I touched you."

She closed her eyes, inhaled. He felt something. This wasn't one-sided. She was right. He felt it too. Her lips curved. She opened her eyes. "What did you want to tell me?"

His lips pursed for a moment. "I had an audition last week. To be the concert pianist for the Greater Chicago Symphony Orchestra. I was the favorite going in. My audition went without flaws. I was sure I had nailed it."

Her heart sank. "What happened?"

"It went to an underdog. A woman not unlike yourself. A modest background. Mostly self-taught at an early age, though she did get a scholarship to an East Coast conservatory and studied there."

"Oh."

He let out a sigh. "And she used to play for a rock band."

"Oh," she said again, understanding dawning.

"I know that doesn't excuse how I treated you. Rejection happens all the time in the music business. I guess you know that."

She nodded. Oh, how she knew that.

He smiled. Her heart skipped. He was so handsome.

"Can you forgive me? I'm really sorry, Jane."

Forgive him? After he'd just given her one of the most precious afternoons of her life? Not to mention the hot threesome they'd just shared. She knew without a doubt she could forgive him almost anything. "Yes, Chandler. I can forgive you."

Was that relief on his face? "Thank God," he said. "There's one more thing..."

"What?"

"I don't want this to be over." His cheeks reddened. "Us, I mean. I want to see you. See where it can lead. I think we could have something amazing together. I..."

Her skin prickled. "What?"

"I think I'm falling in love with you, Janie." He fiddled with a stray lock of blond hair on his brow, looked around the small room, and then locked his gaze with hers. "Fuck. I'm not falling. I'm in love with you. Completely. It happened so quickly. I don't understand it myself. I just know I love you."

She reached for his hand, so warm beneath her touch. "I can't believe you just said those words. I never imagined I'd hear them from you."

His eyes sank just a little. "Are you feeling anything close to the same?" His voice cracked.

Warmth surged to the tips of her toes. "I'm feeling a lot of the same. I think you're phenomenal."

"And?" His eyebrows arched. Was that fear she saw on his face?

"I love you too, Chandler."

He exhaled. "Really? After I was so horrible to you?"

"You weren't horrible to me when we were making love." She touched his cheek. His blond stubble scraped her palm. "And we *were* making love. It wasn't just a fuck like you said."

"No it wasn't. I knew it then. I was being a jerk." He pressed a moist kiss to her fingers. "I love you, Jane Rock."

"I love you, Chandler Hamilton." His warm lips curved against her fingers. "And one more thing..."

"Okay."

"No more Ryan. I'm done sharing you."

Happiness hit her in the gut like a lightning strike. "I think Ryan's great, but I'm okay with that."

His grin lit up his face. "And there's one more thing..."

She shook her head, rolled her eyes. "How many more 'one more things' are there, Chandler?"

"Last one, I promise."

"What is it this time?" He smiled, leaned forward, and brushed his lips lightly over hers. "Let's go wow that agent."

MESSAGE FROM HELEN HARDT

Dear Reader,

Thank you for reading *Her Two Lovers*. If you want to find out about my current backlist and future releases, please like my Facebook page: facebook.com/HelenHardt and join my mailing list: helenhardt.com/signup/. I often do giveaways. If you're a fan and would like to join my street team to help spread the word about my books, you can do so here: facebook.com/groups/hardtandsoul/. I regularly do awesome giveaways for my street team members.

If you enjoyed the story, please take the time to leave a review on a site like Amazon or Goodreads. I welcome all feedback.

I wish you all the best!

Helen

ALSO BY HELEN HARDT

The Misadventures Series
Misadventures of a Good Wife

The Sex and the Season Series
Lily and the Duke
Rose in Bloom
Lady Alexandra's Lover
Sophie's Voice
The Perils of Patricia (Coming Soon)

The Temptation Saga:
Tempting Dusty
Teasing Annie
Taking Catie
Taming Angelina
Treasuring Amber
Trusting Sydney
Tantalizing Maria

The Steel Brothers Saga
Craving
Obsession
Possession
Melt
Burn
Surrender
Shattered (Coming August 29th, 2017)
Twisted (December 26th, 2017)

Other Works
Destination Desire
The Daughters of the Prairie Series
Her Two Lovers

ABOUT THE AUTHOR

#1 *New York Times* and *USA Today* Bestselling author Helen Hardt's passion for the written word began with the books her mother read to her at bedtime. She wrote her first story at age six and hasn't stopped since. In addition to being an award winning author of contemporary and historical romance and erotica, she's a mother, a black belt in Taekwondo, a grammar geek, an appreciator of fine red wine, and a lover of Ben and Jerry's ice cream. She writes from her home in Colorado, where she lives with her family. Helen loves to hear from readers.

Visit her here:

www.facebook.com/HelenHardt

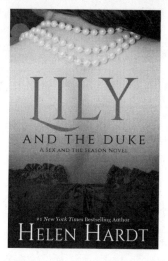

MISADVENTURES OF A GOOD WIFE
THE MISADVENTURES SERIES

Kate and Price Lewis had the perfect marriage—love, fulfilling careers, and a great apartment in the city. But when Price's work takes him overseas and his plane goes down, their happily-ever-after goes down with it.

A year later, Kate is still trying to cope. She's tied to her grief as tightly as she was bound to Price. When her sister-in-law coaxes her into an extended girls' trip—three weeks on a remote Caribbean island—Kate agrees. At a villa as secluded as the island, they're the only people in sight, until Kate sees a ghost walking toward them on the beach. Price is alive.

Their reunion is anything but picture perfect. Kate has been loyal to the husband she thought was dead, but she needs answers. What she gets instead is a cryptic proposal—go back home in three weeks, or disappear with Price...forever.

Emotions run high, passions burn bright, and Kate faces an impossible choice. Can Price win back his wife? Or will his secrets tear them apart?

Visit Misadventures.com for more information!